SHIP OF FOOLS

Cathy Yardley

Copyright © 2019 by Cathy Wilson

All rights reserved.

No portion of this book may be reproduced in any form without written permission from the publisher or author, except as permitted by U.S. copyright law.

contents

1. CHAPTER 1 — 1
2. CHAPTER 2 — 24
3. CHAPTER 3 — 45
4. CHAPTER 4 — 68
5. CHAPTER 5 — 85
6. CHAPTER 6 — 106
7. CHAPTER 7 — 127
8. CHAPTER 8 — 151
9. CHAPTER 9 — 170
10. CHAPTER 10 — 192
11. CHAPTER 11 — 210
12. EPILOGUE — 226

A Note From Cathy — 232

About the Author	234
Let's Get Social!	235
Also By	236

CHAPTER 1

Rachel Frost's head was pounding as she sat on her bed, surrounded by text books and notepads. She rubbed at the webbing between her thumb and forefinger, searching for the acupressure point that might help her head off a migraine. She didn't think that was what was brewing, but she didn't want to risk it, either. There was a quiz in her marketing strategy class at the end of the week that she needed to be ready for, and she wasn't going to let a stress headache get in the way of studying.

Only six months to graduation, she thought with a weak grin. After two and a half years of pursuing her MBA on top of her day job and working with her sisters at the family book and collectibles store, she was feeling a little crispy around the edges, but at least the end was in sight.

Of course, that was not including the latest curveball. Their landlord wanted to take advantage of the skyrocketing housing prices in the area before they inevitably fell back to earth... which meant he was selling the house out from under them unless they could figure out a way to get him to sell to them. The headache throbbed at the thought.

She wasn't sure how she was going to get the money. Her sister Hailey's boyfriend was a famous actor who had more than enough money to buy the house, but their landlord hated actors in general, and his show in particular, and was giving them a hard time. Rachel's other sister, Cressida, was pursuing a wild hair and had actually battled her agoraphobia to travel down to California in pursuit of a treasure a famous author had supposedly hidden there.

Honestly. A *treasure*. Rachel pressed her fingertips against her temples, rubbing in small circles. She loved Cressida and wanted to be as supportive as possible, but she still worried. Cressida was the main reason she wanted to keep the house. It was the only safe space Cressida had ever known – her home base, and the one place that kept Cressida's panic attacks at bay. If they moved, it would be hard for Cressida to re-establish that feeling of safety. Rachel felt sure that Cressida could manage it... eventually. But there would be a painful adjustment curve.

That was what was driving Cressida on this wild goose chase. She was a grown woman, and Rachel couldn't and wouldn't stop her, even though she'd gone hundreds of miles away with a relative stranger – some guy named Noah.

Rachel glanced at her phone. Cressida was supposed to check in with them every day. So far, she hadn't called in yet. Rachel felt the pain in her head ratchet up.

Focus on what you can control, she lectured herself, picking up the marketing strategy book.

After an hour, and a few chapters of *Good Strategy, Bad Strategy* outlined, she was about ready to throw in the towel when the phone finally rang. She looked at the display.

It wasn't Cressida, she realized immediately. But the number was from California.

Maybe it's a telemarketer, she told herself, even as her heart started beating faster. Because in her heart, she knew it wasn't some scam call, wasn't a bot offering her a vacation if she took a survey.

Something's wrong. The tiny voice in her head was fearful, insistent.

She quickly hit "answer." "Hello?"

"Hello," a brisk female voice said. "Who am I speaking with?"

"This is Rachel. Rachel Frost." Her heart started hammering. "Who is this?"

"I'm a nurse at St. Catarina's, in Barstow."

Just like that, Rachel's stomach felt like she was on a roller coaster. *Nurse?*

"You're listed as emergency contact for the owner of this phone. I don't have her name..."

"Does she have red hair? Pale skin?" Rachel didn't even wait for a response. "That's Cressida Frost, my sister."

There was a pause and a muffled response, then the nurse got back on the phone. "Well, Cressida was found out in the desert. We're going to have our doctor look her over, and we'll see about settling her down. We might need an evaluation..."

"Evaluation?" Rachel interrupted. "You mean, psychiatric? Because she's agoraphobic. She's been evaluated here, in Seattle. Well, near Seattle," she amended, then realized she was babbling. "She'll be fine as soon as she gets home. We just need to get her home."

"We'll have to see," the nurse said, and Rachel felt a stab of panic. They needed to move it. Cressida was probably in agony. Being subjected to another psych eval in a strange town was hardly going to help with that, and prolonging her absence from her safe space would only make it worse.

What the hell happened out there?

"Can I talk to her?" Rachel asked.

"I'll have her call you when the panic attack settles down." The woman sounded no-nonsense, although not unkind.

"As soon as you can. Please," Rachel added. "And thank you for taking care of her. We'll be there as soon as we possibly can."

"Yes, all right," the woman answered. "Thank you." She hung up.

Rachel sat still for a second, her mind swirling like a tornado. St. Catarina's in Barstow, she thought. They had to get down there. It would take hours to drive down there – two days, maybe a day and a half if they pushed it. A plane would be better. They needed to take a plane.

They. She needed to let Hailey know. When Rachel's mother had abandoned her as a baby, she'd gotten pregnant with Hailey a few years later, and Hailey had grown up in the foster system after their mother's death. Hailey had found Cressida in a particularly horrific foster home, and the two were close in ways that Rachel knew she'd never fully understand. She had to let Hailey know.

Unfortunately, Hailey wasn't in the house at the moment. She was currently spending the night as she usually did, with her boyfriend, the hot actor Jake Windlass. Rachel quickly hit Hailey's contact number.

"What's up?" Hailey answered immediately. "Thought you had a hot date with some study materials."

"Cressida," Rachel said immediately, then relayed the brief conversation she'd had with the nurse.

"*Fuck!*" Hailey shouted. "When I find the guy who convinced her to go on this fucking treasure hunt, I am going to skin him alive. If she's hurt, I'm going to…"

"I agree, but now's not the time," Rachel said, heading Hailey off before she could go full meltdown. "They'll call if there's anything else wrong with her, but at least it sounds like she's had a massive panic attack. The sooner we can get her home, the better."

"You're right. Okay." There was a second of silence. "Barstow. That's out in the desert. I'm not sure what airports are closest. We'd probably have to go to a major airport and drive. LAX, maybe? Vegas?"

"That's going to take time," Rachel said, gripping the phone tight enough for her fingers to hurt. "Then there's getting Cressida through a crowded airport and onto a crowded passenger plane. After she may have had another psych evaluation."

"We can have them prescribe tranquilizers, then drive her," Hailey said, and Rachel could hear the grimace in her voice. "It's not ideal, but it worked when we moved her from L.A. up to Snoqualmie, remember?"

"Yeah." Of course, Cressida had been barely a teen them. Rachel frowned. Cressida had managed to make it down the coast in the R.V. God only knew where *that* was. Had Noah abandoned Cressida out in the desert?

"Huh? Hold on a second, Jake has a suggestion." There was muffled conversation, then Hailey popped back on the line. "He said that maybe we could use a private plane. That way, they can land at a smaller air strip, closer to Barstow, and it'll get Cressida home more quickly, without dealing with all the crowds and the major airport."

"God, that sounds perfect," Rachel said immediately, gratitude pouring through her.

More muffled conversation. "It might take a day or two to set up the rental, though," Hailey admitted.

Rachel's optimism sank. "Well, that's not ideal," she said. "But it's still a better idea than any we've come up with."

"Jake's going to ask his agent if she knows anybody that's ready to roll," Hailey said, but her voice sounded doubtful. "Worst case scenario, we call first thing in the morning."

"I'll go to SeaTac, hop on a flight to Vegas now," Rachel said. "I could be there by morning, I think."

"We can make this work," Hailey said. "Don't panic. If I could get a private plane there tonight, I would, you know that. I'd do anything for Cressida, or for you. Absolutely anything."

"I know." Rachel bit her lip, feeling guilt wash over her. Not that it was her fault – again, Cressida was a grown woman. But the thought of her adopted sister in pain and alone was enough to send her into a frenzy.

"Hang in there, and tell me what flight you're going on," Hailey said. "If I can find a private flight that's available tonight, I'll let you know. And if you know anybody with a plane – maybe one of the high rollers from the casino? – then you call me, okay?"

She knew Hailey meant it as a joke. Rachel's day job was in the events and marketing department at the Blue Moon Casino, near their house. She wasn't exactly rubbing elbows with the whales that frequented the big-money games. "I'll see if I can think of anyone," Rachel still said, wracking her brain as Hailey hung up.

She could ask her boss if *he* knew anybody... if any of the high rollers had a private plane they might be willing to lend. Although how would she pay back something like that? Other than the casino, the only rich people she knew were her friend Stacy's boyfriend, who did charter jets from time to time when visiting his family in England... and of course, the other actors on Hailey's boyfriend's show, which Hailey would be looking into now...

Ren.

She blinked.

Ren Chu. Her high school boyfriend – and son of one of the wealthiest families in Seattle, owning a conglomerate that provided electronics parts of various sorts for computers, phones, and a wide assortment of gadgetry.

His family owned a plane. Hell, when she knew him, they owned several.

She hadn't given him conscious thought in years, since he'd dumped her unceremoniously the summer after their senior year of high school.

After asking you to marry him the year before.

She closed her eyes. It had hurt, more than anything she'd ever experienced before – or since, if she was being honest. But he'd said one thing before he left.

If you ever need anything, call me. No matter what, no matter when.

For all she knew, he'd changed his phone number. But she still found herself dialing his number – how the hell she remembered it, she had no idea – and paced around her bedroom, her palms getting sweaty, her body bouncing with energy.

"Hello?"

She swallowed hard. *Oh my God, it's him.* She'd know that deep, silky voice anywhere.

"H-hello," she said, cursing her bobble. "Ren?"

"Yes?" He sounded puzzled.

"It's me. Rachel."

There was a pause on the other end of the line. "Rachel?"

She bit her lip. "Rachel Frost," she said, her voice a little tart.

He laughed. "I knew which Rachel," he said, still sounding amused. "I'm just surprised you called."

"You and me both," she said. She sounded breathless to her own ears.

"I'm glad you did," he added. "How are things? You doing all right?"

She didn't have time for small talk. She squinched her eyes shut, like she was about to leap off a high dive.

Then she leaped.

"Remember when you said if I ever needed anything, you'd help me?"

"Yes," he said without hesitation. "Are you all right?" he repeated, this time with more emphasis.

"I need your help," she said. "Specifically, I need your plane."

· ♥ · ♥ · ♥ · ♥ · ♥ ·

It's Rachel.

Ren Chu stood outside of the Hilton hotel in Seattle, temporarily gobsmacked. It was raining, with just a hint of hail, as he stood under an awning, watching the drops fall in strong rivulets. The January air was cold, but the hotel ballroom where the fundraiser he was attending was being held had been hot and stifling, so the cold air felt like a relief.

He hadn't planned on answering his phone, since he didn't recognize the number, but something had prompted him to pick up. On hearing her voice, he'd quickly moved outside to hear her better – to catch every word.

Rachel. Rachel Frost.

My Rachel.

Not that he had any right to think that. They'd broken up, what, ten years ago? Back in high school, for God's sake. He forced himself to focus. "You need... my plane?" he repeated, trying to make sure he understood what she was asking for.

"Yes." He heard her taking a deep breath, then the words tumbled out like water from a waterfall. "Cressida went on this crazy treasure hunt, and now she's stuck in the Mojave Desert. Well, Barstow, really. And she's in the hospital freaking out, and they want to do a psychiatric evaluation, and she's all alone, and I'm trying to get her back as quickly and easily as possible."

He felt stunned as he tried to process what she was saying. "Cressida went on a treasure hunt?" he echoed. "I thought she had agoraphobia...?"

"She does. It's a long story," Rachel said, and he got the feeling she didn't have time to go into details. She sounded panicked, and she so rarely did. Even when they were teens, she'd always had her act together. It took a lot to rattle her.

Like you dumping her.

He winced at the thought.

"You don't need to tell me now," he said, conscious of the fact that he was leaving the door open for her to tell him later. "She's in Barstow, you say?"

"Yes. At St. Catarina's hospital."

"All right." His mind raced, thinking logistics. "I'll contact my assistant, put him in contact with you. He'll make sure that you have a driver that can take you to the private air strip in SeaTac. It's easier than trying to tell you how to get there yourself," he added, when he heard her start to protest. "He'll also get the flight plan together to the closest airfield to the hospital. I'll also arrange for a driver on the other side, one that will pick you up and take you to the hospital. The plane's gassed up and ready to go. I'll have the pilot ready to go in under an hour or two."

He heard her breath hitch. "That's... thank you, Ren. Thank you. The sooner we can get to her, the better."

We?

He hadn't thought about that. Was she maybe bringing a boyfriend? Or... a husband? He felt bile churn. He hadn't thought of that possibility.

Jealousy he had absolutely no right to feel hit him like a kick from Connor Macgregor. He gritted his teeth. "How many of you will be on the flight?"

"Just me and Hailey on the way down," she said. "Maybe Hailey's boyfriend Jake, as well, if that's all right. Then all of us and Cressida on the way back."

Relief coursed through him. "That's fine," he reassured her. "The driver will take you all back after you return to Seattle, okay?"

"That's so much trouble, Ren."

He felt his chest squeeze. *It's not too much trouble for you.*

He knew better than to say it aloud. "This will be the easiest thing for Cressida," he said, knowing that was the most effective approach to get around Rachel's misgivings. "And it'll get you there the quickest."

There was a long pause, and she sighed in acquiescence. "All right. But I'll owe you, big time."

"It's the least I can do," he said, lowering his voice. "Really. I'm happy to help."

"But I'll want to pay you back," she pressed.

He closed his eyes. He didn't want that. He didn't want helping her to seem transactional in any way. He cared about her too much. Even after all this time.

"Why don't you just take care of Cressida," he said gently. "When things settle down, you can call me, and we'll... talk about it. Okay?"

"All right." Rachel's voice sounded scratchy, like she was fighting tears. "Thank you, again."

"We'll talk soon."

She hung up. He stared at the phone for a long moment, memories washing over him. Rachel, wearing glasses and braces, when he'd first fallen head over heels for her in middle school. Freshman year of high school, when they'd started cautiously dancing around a relationship. Sophomore year, their first kiss, their first true acknowledgment of how they felt about each other.

The summer after junior year, and his ill-conceived "secret" proposal.

Then senior year... and the train wreck of their break-up.

Rachel, we're going to be on opposite coasts, and I'm going to have to study and work all the time...

He closed his eyes, thinking of the stupidity. Yeah, they'd been young, and maybe they wouldn't have worked out. But the pain in her eyes, her soft plea that maybe, somehow, they could make it work...

And he'd just walked away from her. *Like an idiot.*

She had never contacted him since. He'd been foolishly sentimental in keeping his phone number the same over all these years, and until tonight, he hadn't realized why.

It was in case Rachel ever decided to reach out. If she'd ever needed anything.

And tonight, she had.

He called his assistant, Stephen.

"Hey Ren," Stephen said. "Thought you were at the fundraiser. Everything okay?"

"I'm still here," Ren said quickly. "I know you're off the clock, but I need you to work some miracles for me."

"It's what you pay me the big bucks for," Stephen said, and Ren could hear his knuckles cracking. "What d'ya need?"

Ren quickly laid out what he told Rachel: the drivers, the plane, picking up Cressida. He could hear Stephen's pen scratching across paper.

"Got it," Stephen said. "Anything else?"

"Just get it done as quickly as possible. The sooner we can get this girl back home, the better."

"Don't worry, I'm on it."

He hung up. It was the best he could do, even though he felt a nervous twist. The Frost sisters were as taken care of as he was humanly able to provide, but until they were back home safe, he knew he'd be feeling the nerves.

He headed back through the doors, reentering the humid ballroom. But his mind wasn't there.

She called me.

When he'd dumped her ten years ago, he'd felt pressured. His parents had made it clear: he had to focus on his studies. He was too young to get married. He'd be too busy to carry on a relationship with a girl three thousand miles away. He'd believed them – and then harshly broken up with the one girl he'd felt an incredible connection with.

When he watched her freeze, fighting tears, he'd told her that she could call him if she ever needed anything. He'd wanted to take it all back.

Instead, she'd said in a numb voice that she didn't want to hear from him ever again. When he told her that the door was always open, she made it clear that it'd be a cold day in hell before she contacted him.

Now, hell had frozen over. She'd called him. She *needed* him.

He was going to help her. He wasn't going to pressure her or use his favor as leverage. But at the same time, he damned well wasn't going to let this opportunity pass him by.

· ♥ · ♥ · ♥ · ♥ · ♥ ·

One month later, Rachel felt an entirely different emotion coursing through her.

"Congratulations!" Rachel said, along with everyone else in the bookstore's "living room", the main selling floor, a room filled with books, memorabilia, games, and of course a few chairs and a couch around a coffee table.

There was a pop as Jake opened champagne in the kitchen. Rachel gave Cressida a hug, and Hailey put an arm around Cressida's slim shoulders. Their sister was radiant, her smile like a thousand-kilowatt flashlight.

"I can't believe I own a house. Our house," she said, and she did sound dazed. "I've never signed so many papers in my life."

"I still can't believe you found a treasure," Hailey said, shaking her head as Jake distributed champagne flutes. "I mean honestly. Who does that?"

"Seriously, though. Up to this point, the biggest investment I've ever made was my laptop," Cressida said, her eyes wide. "I can't believe it. No more landlord or rising rents." She swallowed. "No more worries about having to move."

Rachel looked down at the glass of champagne in her hand. It had been Cressida's agoraphobia that had prompted her on her wild trip to find hidden treasure – one that had not only netted her a fortune but had hooked her up with the man by her side. Noah hovered by her, a small smile playing around his lips. From what they could tell, he was madly in love with her, to the point where he was selling and packing all his stuff in California, just so he could live close to her.

"To Cressida," Rachel said, raising her glass. "For successfully buying a house."

"To Cressida!" They all took a drink, even Cressida, who normally avoided alcohol. She leaned back against Noah, who pressed a kiss against her temple, looking at her tenderly.

"Now we won't have to move the bookstore, either," Hailey said, with an exaggerated sigh of relief. "I was dreading that. We've got so much more inventory now that we've added the collectibles side."

"We're selling a lot more inventory, too, though," Rachel pointed out.

"No, it's a good business move. But half my room is full of Kyla's cosplay costumes that we haven't got space to display," Hailey said. "And we've got those themed board games from various fandoms, too. I'm not going to have room to sleep!"

"It's not like you're sleeping here that much anyway," Rachel pointed out. "You're usually at Jake's."

"That's true." Jake wrapped his arms around Hailey from the back, resting his cheek against hers. "Maybe you can just convert your room to a storage room."

"Ha ha, funny," Hailey said, but she was smiling, and she nuzzled against him.

Rachel felt suddenly and acutely awkward. Cressida was snuggled up with Noah on the couch, sipping champagne. Hailey was enveloped in Jake's embrace. They were both happy couples, both in the full blush of love – Jake and Hailey almost a year now, and Cressida and Noah just a month, but still. It was like being at a New

Year's party and being the only one without someone to kiss.

She drained the rest of her champagne. To her great relief, her phone rang. "I've got to take this," she said, even though for all she knew, it was a scam credit card call. Anything to get away from the cloud of romance.

"Hello?" she said, leaving the room and heading for the stairs.

"Hey. It's Ren."

She stiffened, pausing on a step. "Oh. Um, hi."

Why are you calling?

She didn't want to be rude. He hadn't called, and she hadn't called him, for over a month... not since he'd loaned her the plane. He'd texted her, asking her if Cressida was all right, and she'd given him a brief report of what had happened. But so much had happened in the interim. Cressida getting the treasure officially, and all the shenanigans around buying the house.

And let's face it, she hadn't known what to say to him. Although "thank you" ought to top the list.

"I'm so sorry I haven't called," Rachel said immediately. "I got caught up in stuff over here."

"Is Cressida all right?"

She smiled, touched at his thoughtfulness. She kept ascending, going up all three flights to get to her bedroom. "Yes. She's doing very well. I don't think she'll be leaving the house again any time soon, but... well, you know that treasure I was telling you about? The one she was hunting for?"

"The one that famous author hid?" He said. "I looked into that. I couldn't believe that was a thing."

"Not only was it a thing, she *found* it." She laughed. "She used the money to buy our house."

"No shit?" Ren chuckled. "That's fantastic. That's possibly the coolest thing I've ever heard of."

"I know, right?" Rachel entered her bedroom, closing the door behind her. She wasn't quite sure why. "Listen, I want to thank you. I owe you big time for the use of your plane."

"Really. It was nothing."

"It was something," she countered, emphasizing each word. "We could've gotten Cressida out in a lot of other ways, but... I panicked. I wanted to get her home as soon as possible. I was scared, and I was desperate, and you made everything easy."

"It was the least I could do."

"I don't think you'll ever know just how much that night meant to me," she said. "I want to pay you back."

She heard him let out a long sigh. "Rachel, I was an asshole when we broke up in high school. Trust me when I say that helping out you and your sister was *literally* the least thing I could do."

She blinked. Of all the things he could've said, that was one she wasn't expecting. Still, the sting of the memory hit her unexpectedly.

Long distance relationships don't work, Rachel. Besides, I'm going to be too busy for you.

She winced. Even after all this time.

"The one thing doesn't have to do with the other," she said. "You were kind, and thoughtful, and generous. And I'm happy to repay you." She'd swallow her pride and ask Cressida for the money if she had to.

"You don't need to ask Cressida for the money," he said, reading her mind.

"I just hate feeling indebted."

"There is one thing you could do for me," he said, and she noticed a note of hesitation in his voice.

She felt immediately wary. "What is it?"

"You could go out to dinner with me," he said. "Tomorrow night sound good?"

For a second, her mind went completely blank.

"Dinner?" she repeated. "With you?"

He chuckled again. "Yes. You know. That thing where you eat at night?"

"But... why?"

"I thought we could catch up," he said. "It's been ten years since we spoke. I want to know what's been going on in your life. What you're doing. What's going on."

She still couldn't quite wrap her head around *why*. "Uh..."

"I don't want you to feel pressured, though," he added quickly. "I mean it. The plane ride was no big deal. We have the plane gassed up and ready to go all the time.

It was easy. My Dad uses it all the time to go down to Vegas, spur of the moment. He says that the Pai Gow is better down there."

She grinned. "Tell him the Pai Gow at our casino is actually pretty decent."

She thought she could hear the responding smile in his voice. "The bottom line is, if you go out with me – for dinner, I mean – I want you to go because you want to."

She froze, her hand tightening on the phone.

Did she want to go to dinner with Ren?

He'd broken her heart.

Then again, she'd been eighteen.

He'd asked her to marry him, then dumped her unceremoniously when he went off to college.

But she'd had a decade to process.

You're still hurting.

No, she corrected herself. She was still *pissed*. But she'd gotten over it to ask him for the use of his plane – and he'd given it to her, no questions asked. He'd helped her and her family when she'd needed it.

Maybe, just *maybe*, she was curious about how he'd turned out. What he was doing.

It wouldn't go any further than that.

She swallowed hard, then cleared her throat. "I guess I could do dinner," she said, and hated the breathy note in her voice. She cleared her throat again. "To catch up."

"Great." There was warmth in his voice, rich and sweet, like a mocha.

God, she loved mochas.

"How about tomorrow, seven o'clock, at the Seastar in Bellevue? Want me to pick you up?"

"No, I'll meet you there," she said quickly. It was easier to keep it "just friends catching up" if she had her own car.

"All right. Rachel?"

"Yeah?"

"I'm really looking forward to this."

She laughed hesitantly. "Well, I'll see you tomorrow."

She hung up the phone, then stared at it for a second.

What the hell had she just done?

She made her way downstairs, back to the impromptu party. Noah and Jake were discussing *Mystics*, the show that Jake starred in. Cressida and Hailey were eating cookies and talking about planned renovations, now that the house was theirs.

"I'm thinking of remodeling the kitchen a little," Cressida said, then looked over at Rachel. "Everything all right?"

"Hmm? Oh, sure. Everything's fine," she said quickly. She briefly considered telling them: *I'm going out to dinner with Ren.*

But they remembered what had happened when he'd dumped her, all those years ago. They'd probably tell her how stupid she was being.

Better not to tell them, she thought, and grabbed a cookie. It was just curiosity.

She realized that she hadn't seen him in ten years – and he hadn't seen her.

She smiled slowly.

Curiosity... and maybe just a little bit of payback.

CHAPTER 2

The next night, Ren waited nervously at the bar at the Seastar restaurant. He hadn't been there in years, but he knew that seafood was one of Rachel's favorite things. He bet that she didn't indulge that often – she usually said that seafood was reserved for special occasions.

Okay. He was trying to impress her. He tugged nervously at his tie, then took a fortifying pull from the pale ale he'd ordered, keeping an eye on the door.

Had she changed much?

He had a full docket at work that he ought to be focusing on. They were having problems in their Zhuhai facility, and they were having troubles with some sales and inventory software. He was trying to put out fires daily. He told himself that he hadn't social media stalked Rachel out of a respect for her privacy, but honestly, it had also been a sheer lack of time.

SHIP OF FOOLS

Now, he was wondering if he was setting himself up for disaster. He remembered her as a sweet, nerdy, lovely young woman who "got" him. Hell, he'd loved her enough to ask her to marry him, although he'd been seventeen and probably hormonal at the time. What if she'd changed?

He lifted his beer to take another long chug from the bottle, but his hand froze halfway to his mouth.

She stepped in, unbuttoning her royal purple coat. She was wearing a little black sheathe dress, simple yet stunning, emphasizing her curves while still being minimalistic. Her long black hair cascaded around her shoulders in graceful waves. Her lips were still full and pillowy, painted a deep maroon. Her violet eyes, no longer hiding behind glasses, were wide and doe-like.

She had been beautiful as a teenager. Now, she was a knock-out.

"Ren?" she asked hesitantly.

It was that shy smile that he remembered. All that was missing was...

She bit her lower lip.

He suppressed a groan. Yes, this was Rachel, all right.

He was on his feet, noting with irritation that other men at the bar were staring at her in open and somewhat leering admiration. "Rachel," he said. "How are you?"

It felt like the most natural thing in the world to hug her, gently, gingerly. She pressed her cheek against his, quickly. He took a deep breath of her perfume. It was something flowery, exotic, with a hint of spice. She smelled delicious.

"It's good to see you," she responded, pulling away. Then she bit her lip again. "And a little weird."

He guided her gently, his hand on her lower back – but not too low. They followed the hostess to their table. "Why is it weird?" he asked, as they settled in.

"I haven't seen you in ten years," she said, with a delicate shrug. "A lot can happen in ten years."

"Well, maybe we can start with the highlights, then drill down," he suggested, and was rewarded with a lopsided smirk.

"Smartass," she said. "That hasn't changed."

They looked at their menus, and he surreptitiously snuck peeks at her over the top. "You look amazing," he said finally.

A blush rode high on her cheeks. "Thanks. So do you."

They placed their orders, then surveyed each other. "So. Ten years," Ren said. "What have you been up to?"

She sighed. "Not a whole lot. Went to U Dub for undergrad. Got my degree in Mass Communications. Got a job in event planning and marketing at the casino. Right now, I'm finishing up my MBA, also at U Dub."

"Really? Congrats! You always wanted to get your business degree," he said, remembering her earnestness – her drive. "When do you graduate?"

"June." She smiled at him from under her long lashes.

"That's fantastic." His phone rang, and he cursed softly under his breath. "I'm sorry," he said immediately, then looked at his phone. "It's Jian."

"If it's your brother, of course you should take it," she said, and his chest warmed.

He answered the phone. "What's wrong?"

"Breach of security for the sales software," Jian said without preamble. "Something in the parts ordering, opening a loophole to customer information."

Ren cursed in Mandarin. "Get the software guys in. Now."

"Already on it. Just thought you should know so you can come in."

"I won't be able to do anything until the software guys get a look," Ren said. "But it's probably an update issue. Have them look into when the last software updates went through: if anybody loaded a patch, if there were any bug fixes or roll outs."

"On it. When are you coming in?"

He looked at Rachel. She was taking a sip of her drink, taking in the ambiance of the sand-and-gold colored décor. She looked like a vision.

Maybe I could spend the night with her.

He shook his head, mad at himself. Yes, she was gorgeous, but it was still too early for that kind of thinking. "Give me a few hours," he said, then hung up.

"Everything all right?" Rachel asked, her blue eyes looking at him with concern.

"Business stuff," he said, shrugging.

"*Business stuff*," she echoed, rolling her eyes. "That's non-specific. What have you been up to the past ten years, Ren Chu?"

"Nothing much," he downplayed. "You know I went to Harvard. Got my undergrad and MBA degrees there. Interned at a few places, like Google. Now, I work for the Chu Corporation, mostly with their electronic parts division."

"Sounds important." She nodded, sipping her drink. "You always knew you were going to work for your family someday."

They went silent for a minute. He imagined she was remembering the last time he'd brought it up: when he was breaking up with her, senior year.

I need to focus on school. I'm going to be working for my family, and they don't take failure well. Or at all.

He frowned.

"You're working with your family, too," he said quickly, to change the subject. "Hailey, Cressida... Grandma Frost too?"

The server dropped off their entrees – sea bass for him, seared ahi and some hand rolled sushi for her – and then retreated. Rachel's eyes looked down at her plate, and she let out a deep breath.

"Grandma Frost died four years ago," Rachel said quietly. "Breast cancer. She'd had it since my senior year at U Dub."

"Oh, God. I'm so sorry," he said quickly. "I didn't know."

"Obviously. Why would you?" She shrugged. "It was hard. But we got to spend as much time with her as possible, and we took turns taking her to chemo and radiation and hanging out with her. It brought us closer together as sisters." She paused. "It did mean putting off grad school for a while, but she was adamant that I still go."

He looked at her, feeling admiration radiate through him. "Sounds like you've been through a lot in the past decade."

"Yes," she said simply. Then she looked at him, her expression sad.

Another moment of quiet. "You were always one of the strongest women I knew," he said. "From what you've told me, and what you've gone through, it sounds like you're even stronger now."

Her smile was small but sweet. "Thank you, Ren."

They tucked in to their food, talking about their jobs, their siblings, where they lived. He told her about his condo in Seattle; he was surprised to find that she was still living at the bookstore, although she wasn't sharing a room with Hailey any more… she was situated in Grandma Frost's loft bedroom. "It took a long time to get used to it," she admitted. They talked about their jobs. He was delighted with the addition of collectibles and "nerd memorabilia" to Frost Bookstore.

Best of all, they were joking with each other, still that easy back-and-forth.

Finally, as dessert was being served, he nudged at his crème brulee. "So... have you been seeing anyone?"

She shot him a tiny, sly smile. "You mean in the ten years since we broke up?"

He smiled back ruefully. "Yes."

"There have been a few serious relationships," she said, then sighed. "But right now, no. With school, and work, and the store, I just haven't had the time. Or the interest, really."

So she was single. He could help but feel buoyed by a jolt of excitement. Of course, she'd just said she was too busy for relationships.

Maybe there was wiggle room there? He was busy, too, after all.

"How about you?" she asked, spooning up a bite of tiramisu.

"Still single myself," he said quickly. "I've seen some people in the past ten years, but like you said – a lot's gone on, and I've been really busy."

She nodded.

He grabbed the check over her protests. "I asked you to dinner, so I get the check," he said firmly. "I was wondering... do you think about us at all?"

"What do you mean?"

"You know. About what we used to be like," he said. "About what might've happened, if we had stayed together."

Her expression didn't waver, but her eyes snapped. "It was a long time ago," she said, her voice perfectly even. Too perfect, like she was forcing a sense of calm. "And let's face it, you were right. We were too young. Odds were good we would've crashed and burned in an epic manner."

"But we're not too young now," he murmured. "We've got ten years of experience behind us. We're different people than we were then."

She leaned forward, her voice lowering. "What exactly are you saying, Ren?"

He took a deep breath. "I'm saying," he offered quietly, "have you considered what would happen if we gave it another try? Started seeing each other again?"

She stared at him, those violet eyes like lasers, searing into his soul.

Then she threw back her head and laughed.

· ♥ · ♥ · ♥ · ♥ · ♥ ·

"I take it that means you haven't thought about it," Ren said wryly.

"I haven't considered it because it's... it's..." Rachel shook her head. *Ridiculous? Ludicrous? Unbelievable?* "Inconceivable," she finally settled on.

He grinned. "I do not think that means what you think that means," he said, with Inigo Montoya's accent from *The Princess Bride*.

She couldn't help it. She grinned back. "Unlikely, then."

He leaned closer to her, his dark brown eyes shining. "Tell me why."

She felt her mouth go dry, and quickly took a drink of water.

She thought she'd done a great job tonight. When she'd walked in, she'd managed to stay confident, her head held high. She wasn't going to let the guy who had dumped her ten years ago walk all over her again. She was going to show him what he was missing, in her little black dress and best black stilettos. She'd done her hair and makeup carefully, even though she usually just gave them a careless swipe when she went to work or school. She was a *killer* tonight.

Then she'd gotten a look at him, and she'd felt her walls start to crumble.

He looked fantastic. The years had only been kind to him. His jet-black hair was cut short, putting his sharp cheekbones on display. His dark eyes seemed to eat her up, and his smile – God, that smile! – displayed the dimple that flirted at the left edge of his mouth. He had some laugh lines crinkling at the corners of his eyes that made him look more mature, distinguished.

She wanted to lick him.

None of that, you idiot, she chastised herself, putting on her very best lock-down mode. She was here because he'd asked, and because she wanted to thank him for the use of his plane. But honestly, she was there for one reason, and one reason only.

To show him what he'd walked away from.

She'd managed to do that for the past two hours. She hadn't embarrassed herself by mooning over him or throwing herself at him, as she imagined a lot of women must do on a regular basis. He was a billionaire international business magnate, after all, working for his parents' huge corporation. And he was gorgeous. He managed to make cutting sea bass look ridiculously sexy.

She needed to get out of here.

Then he'd hit her with the "do you ever think about us getting back together?" question, and she couldn't help it: nervous laughter bubbled out of her like a shaken champagne bottle.

"I can honestly say I never, ever considered the possibility of the two of us getting back together," she said, shaking her head.

"But why not?"

"Why not?" She bought time by carefully folding the linen napkin on the table. "How about because I haven't spoken with you in ten years? And because ten years ago, you broke up with me – broke off our *engagement*, in a way that broke my heart?"

She bit her lip. She hadn't meant to say all of that. She quickly cleared her throat, looking up.

"I'm not saying it wasn't the right move. In fact, I agree with you one hundred percent, in hindsight," she said, glad that her voice was even, sure that her expression was placid. "Honestly, if it hadn't been for Cressida and wanting to borrow your plane, I think I never would've seen you again."

"You told me not to get in contact with you," he reminded her. "When we broke up. You said that if you ever wanted to talk to me again, you'd call me. I took that seriously."

"And I appreciate it."

His eyes glowed. "I kept the same damned phone number since high school on the off chance that you might want to talk to me."

She blinked. "That's... surprising."

And crazy. And – she had to admit – sort of romantic.

Hey, he dumped you, remember?

She forced herself to focus. "I still want to pay you back for letting us use your plane," she said, trying to shift them back to a less emotionally charged subject.

"You know it wasn't a big deal for me. And don't you think, on some level, you wanted to reach out to me? You could've figured out another way, but you trusted me," Ren pointed out. "And I'm glad I could help, both because

I care about Cressida, but also because it got me back in contact with you."

She frowned. "We had dinner."

"And I enjoyed it, more than I've enjoyed going out with anyone in a long time."

"It's been ten years," she repeated. "We're really different people now." She paused. "*I'm* a different person now."

He nodded. "I'd like to learn more about those differences. I want to find out all about you."

She stared at him. "Ren, what in the world is bringing this on?"

"What do you mean?" He stared back at her, his gaze intense. "I would think it's clear."

She got up. "I think that maybe you're fetishizing the past a little bit," she said, with a shaky laugh.

He got up in response, then helped her into her thick wool coat. She got a whiff of his cologne. It smelled like something manly and expensive, like cedar and some kind of musk. She wanted to bury her head in the lapel for a second. Just for a second, to really breathe it in.

You have got to get out of here, now, before you do something seriously stupid.

She waited until he got his coat on, and she smiled at him, her best customer-service smile. "Thank you for dinner, Ren," she said. "It's been nice. Odd, but nice."

"Let me walk you to your car," he said, gesturing to the door.

"Um. Okay."

They walked in silence to the parking garage. She could feel the cold February breeze. There was talk that there would be snow soon. She hoped not. They walked in silence to her car, a beat-up Subaru that she'd done her best to clean up. "This is me," she said. "Thanks, again."

He leaned against the car, and in a flash she was reminded of when he'd walk her to her car at school. His smile was quicksilver, his eyes flashing with mischief... the look he gave her before he usually kissed her senseless.

She couldn't help it. Her heart started slamming against her ribcage, her breathing went shallow. She clutched at her purse.

"I missed you." His smile was lopsided. "I didn't realize how much until tonight."

Gaaaaaahhh! Right in the feels!

She fought to keep her expression impassive. "I missed you, too," she said, trying to make it sound less emotional than she was feeling.

"I missed talking to you."

He was leaning close enough that she could feel his body heat, even through her thick coat. "Tonight was fun," she admitted.

He moved closer still, closing the gap between them, until she could feel his breath brushing against the side of her neck. "I'd like to talk to you again," he said. "Would you mind if I called you some time? No pressure."

She shivered, and not because of the cold. Part of her just wanted to reach out and grab him, see if his lips were as firm and pliable as she remembered. It had been a while since she'd had sex, her body was quick to remind her. *It might not hurt to see if other things were as you remembered, is all we're saying.*

She pulled back for a quick second, then took him in.

His nostrils were flared slightly, and she could make out the quick thump of his pulse in his throat. His pupils were dilated. She wasn't the only one affected here.

He wanted her.

This is like playing with dynamite.

Knowing it was stupid, she reached out, ready to give him a quick hug. Only somehow, she forgot to let go. The two of them pressed together near her car, his arms wrapping around her, his head nuzzling the top of hers. She could've sworn she felt him brush the slightest kiss against the crown of her hair.

"You can call me," she heard herself say, as she untangled herself from their sweet, slow embrace. "I mean, if you're not too busy. I know you've got a lot going on with work, and all."

"I'll make time," he said, his voice deep and hypnotic. "Goodnight, Rachel. We'll talk soon."

She nodded, then got into her car, changing her shoes from sexy stilettos to slip-on sneakers. She waited until he walked away, then banged her head gently on her steering wheel.

"Stupid, stupid, stupid," she muttered at herself.

Well, it wasn't that bad. She'd just agreed to *talk* to him again, that was all. And she'd made him want her. He'd gotten a good look at what he was missing.

Of course, does it count if you want him right back?

"Oh, shut up," she said to the empty car, and then started the engine.

· ♥ · ♥ · ♥ · ♥ · ♥ ·

Call her already!

Ren glanced at his watch. It was six o'clock the following day, and he was still at the glass desk in his black-and-gunmetal gray office, trying to focus on work when it was the last thing he really wanted to do.

He'd spent all day putting out fires. He wanted to call Rachel that morning, after spending the night tossing and turning, thinking about her. He hadn't even kissed her, for Christ's sake, but she was traipsing through his mind like a ghost, haunting him.

He didn't want to seem too desperate, but the thing was, he *was* desperate.

There was a knock on his door, and he looked up. His brother, Jian, was standing there, just wearing a dress shirt and tie, no jacket. He looked frazzled. "The software loophole's closed."

"I know. Ted told me this morning," Ren said.

"Yeah, but now it's closed on the audit side," Jian said. "We need to do something about the software developer we've got under contract. It was their screw-up, and it feels like I'm running around like a chicken every time they try to roll a change out, trying to fix their fuck-ups."

"I know," Ren said, rubbing at his temple. "I need to talk with Mom and Dad about canceling their contract. I think we've got the talent in house, or could hire more talent, to develop something that's more nimble. Or we could hire another developer altogether."

Jian sighed, leaning against the door frame. "So where were you last night, anyway? I'm surprised that you weren't here with the developers to pinpoint the problem."

Ren shifted uncomfortably. "I was out. At dinner."

"Well, why couldn't you just box it up and come in?" Jian asked, not comprehending the import of Ren's statement.

"Because I was with a *woman*, dingus," Ren spelled out.

Jian blinked, then grinned. "You? You had a date?"

"I've been known to go on them from time to time."

"Not in the past year. Not since Dad shifted you to being head of I.T. and software development for the Electronics Division," Jian said. "Where the hell did you meet somebody? Don't tell me Mom fixed you up."

Their mother's attempts at match-making were legendary.

"No, Mom didn't fix me up," Ren groused. "If you must know... I was catching up with, um, Rachel Frost."

Now Jian's eyes nearly bugged out of his head. "No. *Shit.*" He started to laugh. "I thought she hated you!"

"Yeah, well, I did her a favor, so she started talking to me again," Ren said. "And we caught up."

"Is she still hot?"

Ren grimaced. "Knock it off."

"What? She's not your girlfriend anymore," Jian replied shamelessly. "And even in high school, even with those dorky glasses – she was bangin'."

"Don't. You don't have the street cred to say 'bangin'' in any context," Ren said with a scowl.

"Fine." Jian rolled his eyes. "Is she *still as beautiful* as she was in high school?"

Ren thought about it. "Even more."

Jian let out a low whistle. "No wonder you're looking like somebody slapped you," he said. "You gonna see her again?"

"If I have anything to say about it," Ren said. "But she's kind of wary."

"Well, you did dump her," Jian said.

"Yes, I know. Thanks for pointing out the obvious," Ren said with a scowl. "I'll make it up to her."

Jian shook his head. "You know what Mom and Dad are going to say."

At that, Ren stiffened. "They don't have anything to do with this."

"Big brother, you're the heir apparent for Chu Enterprises," Jian said. "You've got pressure I don't even want to think of. They've moved you through various divisions, all with an eye towards making you the big daddy of the family empire so our father can go play golf and Pai Gow for the rest of his life. They're not going to want you distracted."

"Mom's been after me to get involved in a relationship forever," Ren protested. "I don't see how this is different."

"It's different because Mom's been trying to get you married to people who are advantageous to the business. Trust fund kids from families who would ally well with Chu Enterprises," Jian said, as if it were patently obvious. "And she's been looking for women who understand that work would have to come first."

Ren frowned. "She hasn't." Had she? He hadn't given his mother's suggestions much credence.

"Well, you wouldn't know because you haven't gone out on the dates," Jian said. "Trust me. After a few fix-ups, I realized that I was basically ticking off boxes in an arranged marriage brochure. And the women? Bored as hell, but they seemed to get what was going on and were on board with it."

Ren felt appalled. "Are you kidding? Why did you even go?"

Jian reddened. "Well, Mom was pushing, and you know how she and Dad get," he temporized. "Besides... dude, I hadn't gone out in months."

It took Ren a second to understand what his brother was getting at. Then he laughed. "You thought you'd get *laid*?"

"I don't get out enough," Jian muttered. "It was worth a shot."

Ren shook his head. Even as work-hammered and clueless as he was, he wouldn't go out with one of his mother's fix-ups with an eye towards hooking up.

"So, did you hit it with Rachel?" Jian pressed.

Ren stood up, advancing on his brother, who held his hands up in defense.

"What! I was just asking."

"Be careful, Jian," Ren said, his voice low. "I still care about Rachel, very much. I'm not just looking for a hook up with her."

Jian studied him carefully for a second, then his jaw dropped. "You're thinking of getting back together with her? Seriously?"

"It's too early to say."

Jian shook his head. "Well, good luck with that," he said, his tone dubious. "Just remember: we've got brand review coming up in a few weeks, we're having problems with the factory in Zhuhai and the software developer stuff there, and we're going to be dealing with a bunch of drama if we get out of the developer contract and need to be pulling in more people in house."

"I know," Jian said.

"That doesn't leave you a lot of room for romancing," Jian added.

"I *know*."

Jian shrugged. "You want to grab some burgers?"

Ren shook his head. "Nah. I'm going to try to get home at a decent hour tonight."

"And call *her*, huh?" Jian shook his head. "You're whipped already, and you've already had one date."

"Says the guy who thinks his mom will get him a hook up," Ren said to Jian's retreating figure. Jian flipped him off, and Ren laughed.

Once Jian had left, Ren cleared off his desk, getting things ready for the morning, and shut down his computer. He'd go home, eat some dinner, and call Rachel. He knew she had full days, too: work, school, the bookstore.

Maybe he should text her, instead. Wasn't that what people did? Maybe he should check in first.

He shot her a quick text.

Ren: *Hey. You busy?*

He waited a few minutes, only to hear her responding ping.

Rachel: *Just got home from the casino. Why?*

Ren: *I was thinking of you. Are you the type that would rather text than talk?*

Rachel: *Depends on who I'm talking with.*

Ren: *It's old fashioned, but I'd like to call you. I like hearing your voice.*

Ren: *Also, I can't use emojis for shit.*

Rachel: *LOL*

Rachel: *Most guys I know have terrible emoji game.*

Ren: *Well, that's something. So can I call you tonight?*

There was a longer pause. He found himself getting impatient as he walked to his car. Finally, he got the message ding.

Rachel: *I need to study tonight.*

He felt disappointment hit him. Was she blowing him off? Or did she really need to study? Maybe he could offer to help. He'd gotten good grades in B-school.

Or would that seem too desperate?

Before he could come up with an answer, another ding sounded.

Rachel: *But if you really want to talk, I'll probably be done around 9:30.*

He let out a breath, a smile cracking his face.

Ren: *Sounds good. Talk to you then.*

He immediately put his phone back in his pocket, climbing into his car. And felt like an idiot.

There were going to be challenges to getting together with Rachel. His parents might not be thrilled, he realized. And he'd have to negotiate how to make time for her when business was pressing. But it was all moot unless he could frickin' *get her to see him again.* That was the objective.

CHAPTER 3

Rachel closed her book and put her notes away, trying to remain casual as she glanced at the clock on her nightstand. Nine-twenty-five.

Ren is going to call.

She shoved the book into her backpack. He might not, she told herself, even though she knew she was lying. She thought about compounding the lie and telling herself she didn't care, but she couldn't go quite that far.

She'd seen him for dinner, and he was expressing interest. And for the life of her, she couldn't understand *why*.

That wasn't a slam on her: she knew that she'd lucked out in the looks department. Plenty of guys from her business program had asked her out, and guys from the casino followed after her on a regular basis. If she wanted a relationship, she could be in one easily.

But Ren was on another level. He was a billionaire, or the son of billionaires. He could see super models if he so desired. And the women that were in his social circle probably had a hell of a lot more going for them than a night class MBA and a ton of school debt, a little family bookstore, and a job at a local casino.

There was also the fact that he'd *had* her. He'd been her first: her first serious boyfriend, first lover. He'd been her world for years. They'd started dating in sophomore year of high school. He'd proposed their junior year.

Then, he'd changed his mind senior year, before he left for Cambridge.

She winced. The pain wasn't as fresh, but it was still *there*, like an infection.

He'd had his chance. What realization was bringing him to her doorstep *now*?

The phone rang, and she let out a little yelp. Frowning, she glanced at the display.

Ren.

She answered it. "Hello?"

"Hey there." He sounded tired. "How are you?"

"I got my studying done." She bit her lip. "Why are you calling?"

"I told you I'd call," he said, sounding surprised. "And I wanted to hear your voice. Why? Is now a bad time?"

"No. Not really." She took a deep breath. "It just... it's odd. Us talking again, after all this time."

"I think it's nice." She heard sounds, like cloth rustling. Was he changing clothes? The thought made her heart rate pick up, just a bit. "What are you studying?"

"Marketing strategy." Did her voice sound huskier than usual? Rougher? *Jeez, get it together*.

"I liked strategy," he said. "Forecasting, and the math behind it, was my downfall. I'm more a big picture guy."

"With the casino, I'm more of a tactician," she admitted. "But the big picture stuff has been useful. If I stay with the casino, I'm sure I could use it, maybe get promoted."

"If you stay?" He sounded curious.

"Well, when I graduate, I might look for something that pays a bit better. Maybe something in the city?"

"I bet you'd kick ass." He sounded approving, and supportive, and it made her chest warm. "You're an intelligent woman. Focused. Anybody could see that, even back in high school."

She felt her cheeks heat in a blush. "Thanks. It's not Harvard, and I don't work at a multi-billion-dollar corporation, but hey, we do what we can."

There was a beat of silence after that statement, and she sighed.

"That came out a touch more bitter than I intended," she said.

"You could've handled Harvard," Ren said. "And I'll bet you could handle working at Chu Enterprises, if you wanted to."

"I don't." The words were blunt, but she didn't feel apologetic. It was a huge conglomerate, and it was prestigious, but it wasn't what she wanted at all. "I might want to get a better job, but I think I'd like a smaller-firm feel."

"Why?"

She stretched out on the bed, holding the phone up to her face. "It's like Frost Fandoms," she said. "I like working with my sisters. I don't know that I'd make it my full-time gig, the way Hailey and Cressida have, but I know that it means a lot more to me because I love them, and I believe in them. I'd want to work somewhere that values what I believe in." She grinned. "Someplace intimate, and, you know, not evil."

She was referring to Google's old mission statement, the one that had stated that they wouldn't be evil. It really broke her heart when they took that out.

He chuckled, obviously getting the reference. "Well, we're not evil, but I don't blame you. Chu Enterprises is huge. I've worked in three divisions now, and they've got their own quirks and bureaucracies."

There it was again. "You sound tired, Ren," she observed. "What's going on?"

"Work stuff." He sighed. "I feel like I've been putting in some long hours lately. We've been having some problems with our sales ordering and inventory software programs, and we're..." He paused. "Sorry. It's boring, technical stuff."

"I could follow along," she said, feeling a little offended.

"Yeah, but I didn't just call you so I could complain about my day," he said. "How's that going to convince you to see me again?"

She paused at that. "Was that the reason you were calling?"

You had that feeling. You knew *why he was calling.*

"I was calling because I like talking with you," he said. "But yes. There was that, too."

She took a deep breath, stretching out, trying to work the tension out of her shoulders. This was crazy, and she ought to shut him down immediately. But it was kind of nice, having him call her up.

"Where are you?" he asked.

"Huh? Oh. I'm in my bedroom."

He let out a strangled sound. "Oh?"

She snickered. "You're dying to ask me what I'm wearing, aren't you?"

"That would be crass." He cleared his throat. "And we haven't hit that point in our relationship yet. But I have high hopes."

She let out a giggle even as her skin heated. He used to ask her what she was wearing, sometimes in a joking manner... sometimes in a serious one that had her panties melting. "If it makes any difference, I'm wearing a parka and a pair of fleece-lined overalls," she lied.

He laughed. "Well, that does it. I'm worked up."

She shook her head. "So that must be why you want to see me again. You can't find girls like this in the big city... ones that can make a thick woolen parka look good."

"You can make anything look good," he said.

She frowned, thrown off her game a little. "What are *you* wearing?"

"I got home early enough to get a workout in," he said matter-of-factly. "So I'm just wearing a T-shirt and sweats."

She thought about him in workout gear, his arm muscles sharply defined. He'd been a soccer player in high school, and had gotten his black belt in Tae Kwon Do. She remembered just how good that body looked after exercise.

Her mouth went dry.

"But I can break out my puffy jacket and a pair of Uggs, just for you," he added. "Tundra sexy. That's us."

She laughed. He'd always been like this: gently goofy.

"When can I see you again?" he said. "I really want to get a good look at this parka of yours."

She felt her breathing go shallow. "What makes you think you get a chance at seeing me in this parka, or anything?" she asked.

"I don't want to rush you, or push you," he said. "But I do want to see you."

"Yes, but *why*?"

"Why wouldn't I?" Ren asked. "You're smart, you're sexy, you're sweet. You're the complete package."

"You don't even know me," she said. "It's been *ten years.* I could be a serial killer for all you know."

"Okay. Are you a serial killer?"

"Like I'd tell you!" She rolled her eyes.

"I'm going to take that as a no." He sounded like he was smiling. "You're right. I know we talked about it over dinner: we've both changed. But there's no way we're going to be able to find out what those differences are unless we see each other again."

She felt temptation pulling at her like a rip tide. Maybe he'd changed over the past ten years. He'd apologized for how he'd broken up with her. He wasn't the same kid, overburdened with parental expectations and a college future three thousand miles away from her.

Maybe he was worse.

She frowned. Did she want to put herself out there?

"I'm not really in the mood for a relationship," she said, and it sounded weak to her own ears.

"I'm willing to wait." He said. "As long as I can still see you, I'm willing to go as slowly as you want, take as much time as you need."

If we start seeing each other, I'm afraid I won't want to go slow.

She squirmed on the bed. "I just… it feels like a stupid idea. People don't start dating their high school sweethearts. It never works out."

"We could," Ren said, his voice low and intense. "What are you doing tomorrow?"

She closed her eyes. *You, if I'm not careful*.

"I have studying to do, so I don't have time to go out." Of course, she was fairly certain she was going to nail that test, but it was the best defense she could come up with.

"Okay."

"Okay?" She frowned.

"Okay. You're too busy to go out tomorrow. I understand."

He was taking that rejection very easily. She was surprised to find herself stung that he wasn't trying for later in the week. "And I've got the quiz later in the week," she said, as if to point out that she was going to be too busy for a while.

"All right." He sounded amused.

"So I guess I'll go to bed now," she said, although it was *far* too early.

"I'll call you again," he said. "If that's okay."

"Whatever," she said, irritation now fully at the fore.

"Hey, Rachel?"

"What?"

She heard the smile in his voice. "Think of me tonight, huh?"

She felt it like a slash. He used to say that, before they hung up. *Think of me tonight.*

"Because I'll think of you." With that, he hung up.

She was struck dumb, unsure if what he'd said was inappropriate. It probably was. But the damnable thing was, she *would* think of him... just like she had the night previous. Just like she had every night since she'd called him to borrow the plane.

Damn him. He was getting under her skin, and she wasn't sure what to do about it.

· ♥ · ♥ · ♥ · ♥ · ♥ ·

Ren hadn't been to the Frost Bookstore – now Frost Fandoms, with a nice sign on the front lawn and over the front door – in ten years. Once he'd broken up with Rachel, he knew that he wouldn't be welcomed back, and he accepted that. In fact, he was pretty sure Hailey had tracked him down and threatened to "castrate him with a melon baller" or similar. Hailey had always had a temper, and he had just broken Rachel's heart.

Still, he kind of hoped Hailey was out of town or something, he thought with a wince.

There had been a few flurries that had turned to sleet, and the already miserable commute from Seattle to Snoqualmie had been a long hour on I-90. Add to that some wait time for the pizza he'd ordered, and it was now around seven-thirty. He hoped Rachel hadn't already eaten, but he knew she was also a sucker for pizza. Who wasn't?

Wincing as he was pelted by the cold and wet, he carefully made his way up to the front door. The sign said the store would be open another half hour. He stepped inside. The lights were warm and inviting, the store itself colorful. There were still tons of books on floor-to-ceiling shelves that flanked the walls and windows. There were also whimsical displays of board games, memorabilia, and costumes from various fandoms.

He couldn't help but look over the stuff. They had a really cool Assassin's Creed costume, he noticed, one that looked about his size. And Jedi robes. Not that he had a lot of places to *wear* a costume, per se. But he'd slam dunk the company Halloween contest.

Okay, so Chu Electronics didn't *have* a Halloween costume contest. But he could start one, couldn't he?

"Can I help you?"

He looked over to see a pretty red-haired woman walk up to him from behind the counter. Her skin was milk-pale, and she had a sprinkling of freckles. She also had a gentle smile.

"Cressida?" he asked. "Is that you?"

She looked puzzled for a moment, then tilted her head as recognition settled in. "*Ren?*"

"Yeah. Hi." He shifted his weight between his feet and adjusted his grip on the pizza boxes. "It's good to see you."

"I'm surprised to see you," she said. Stunned might be the better word, he noticed. She glanced down. "Pizza?"

"Yeah. I understand that Rachel was probably studying tonight, so I thought I'd bring by some pizza, see if she might want any help."

Now Cressida goggled. "*Rachel* knows you're here?"

"Well, she doesn't know... I mean, this is kind of a surprise."

"How do you know she's studying?" Cressida asked. "Wait. You're *stalking* her?"

"What? No!" Ren shook his head. "We talked last night. I had dinner with her the other evening."

"Really." Cressida was a sweet kid, he remembered, and she inherently believed in people. That said, he could tell she was having difficulty believing what he was saying. "Well. Let me, um, get her."

He waited, looking at some of the other merchandise. A few other people were browsing, as well. It looked like the store was doing all right.

To his surprise, Rachel came out flanked by Hailey, who was glaring daggers at him. He took a cautious step back.

"Hey there," he said, with forced casualness. "I brought pizza."

Rachel looked at him like she couldn't believe he was there. Hailey growled at him low in her throat.

"That's... what are you doing here?"

"You're studying," he said. "At least, that's what you said last night, so you couldn't go out. I figured if you couldn't go out, I could at least bring some food in. You still like pizza, right?"

"Who doesn't like pizza?" she said, echoing his thoughts. He smiled.

Hailey looked at her, then at him, then back at Rachel. "That's what you said *last night*?"

"We talked on the phone, yes," Rachel said, and he saw the blush hit her cheeks.

"Anything else?"

"Not that it's any of your business," Rachel said, her tone cool, "but we went out to dinner the other night."

"Dinner?"

Rachel rolled her eyes.

Hailey looked around the store. "You are so lucky that there are other customers in here, pal," she said, her tone low and dangerous.

"*Hailey*," Rachel hissed. "It's fine, okay? We just caught up. It's no big deal."

"Oh yeah? Then why is he here with pizza?"

"So we can eat?" Rachel said.

"Oh, don't be naïve," Hailey said. "He wants something."

Ren finally felt his irritation bubble up. "*He* is also standing right here," he said, forcing his voice to stay mild. "But mostly *he* wants to have dinner with Rachel and maybe help her with some marketing strategy, if she needs a study buddy."

"You had a chance to be a buddy ten years ago," Hailey pointed out.

"I've apologized," he said. "Though, as Rachel pointed out, it's not your business. I am trying to make amends."

Hailey looked at Rachel. "And… you're okay with this?"

"It's no big deal," Rachel said, and for a second, he believed it. She sounded almost bored. "I mean, bringing pizza was really thoughtful, Ren. I appreciate it. And I'm not going to turn down some help with this quiz, if you want to help out a bit."

"I don't mind at all."

"Come on, let's go to the kitchen." They walked past Hailey and Cressida, who was watching with wide eyes. He put down the pizza boxes on the counter, then they helped themselves to slices.

"You remembered I love Hawaiian," Rachel said, with a small smile.

Hailey followed them in, as did Cressida. "I'm grabbing some of this meat special pizza," Hailey said, still staring at him suspiciously.

"I brought some for everybody," Ren said easily.

She grabbed a piece, then gave the *I'm watching you* expression. Rachel shook her head.

"I'm sorry. She just remembers what it was like… you know, back then." Her doe eyes were solemn. "I was kind of a wreck for a while, and she tends to hold a grudge."

Guilt stabbed at him.

She ate her pizza, looking pensive, then looked at him. "I'll let you help me study," she said. "I missed being your friend."

He swallowed, and it had nothing to do with the pizza he was eating. "I missed you, too," he said, his voice thick with emotion.

"But it's just friendship," she said, and her tone was sorrowful.

He paused a beat, looking at the door. The sisters were helping customers before the store closed. He wished he could have this conversation in more of a private setting. "Why?" he pressed. "Why just friendship?"

"We've already talked about this."

"You've given me reasons for why you're nervous about it," he admitted. "But there are solutions to those reasons. And I wonder why you couldn't give me – us – another chance."

She bit her full lower lip. God, what he wouldn't give to be able to do the same.

"I can go slowly," he reiterated. "I told you, I'll do what it takes."

Her forehead furrowed slightly. "You'd do whatever it took? What if I gave you some... I don't know, Herculean labors?"

He laughed. "You wouldn't."

"It's been ten years," she said, and her eyes lit ruefully. "Maybe I've changed, and developed a dark side."

"Okay, do you have any chores for me?"

She looked at the ceiling as if she were considering it, then shook her head. "I'm not the type to come up with some kind of vengeance plan," she said, shaking her head.

"I know." He smiled.

"Although I could ask for Hailey's help," she pointed out. "And Cressida's surprisingly creative when you piss her off."

He felt his stomach knot. "That's... disturbing."

She laughed. "You're here, anyway. I have an early morning tomorrow, so you can't stay that long, but if you're serious about helping me study, I'll take it."

"All right." He helped clear away their dishes, then looked at her. "Where do you want to study?"

"All right, the store's closed," Hailey said, coming into the kitchen with Cressida.

"I'm going to make some dinner for Noah, when he gets off shift," Cressida said, looking at Rachel.

"He can have some pizza," Ren offered, remembering Rachel had mentioned Cressida's boyfriend.

"That's nice of you."

"We're just going up to my room to study," Rachel said.

There was a moment of silence, and Ren felt his heart accelerate. It was déjà vu, just like high school. Only back then, if they could go up to a room by themselves the last thing they'd do was *study.*

Damn it, she means "study" this time!

He was berating himself, ready to follow Rachel, when Hailey held his arm, holding him back as Rachel began ascending the stairs.

"It was cool of you to loan us your plane," Hailey said begrudgingly. "But if you're trying to leverage that into getting back into Rachel's pants, I am going to beat some goddamn sense into you."

He stared at her. "Jesus, Hailey," he said, shocked. "What kind of person do you think I am?"

"I don't know, do I?" she snapped. "All I know is, after ten years, you're suddenly taking her out to dinner, bringing pizza by? Offering to help her 'study'?" Hailey scoffed. "You *broke her fucking heart*. She cried for months over you. And she still hasn't gotten over it. If you're here, you'd better be fucking serious."

"I am serious," he said sharply. "How far we go is up to her, but I'm in this. All the way."

Hailey stared at him, as if studying him. Then she nodded.

"Just don't hurt her," Hailey said somberly.

"I won't," he promised, then quickly went to follow Rachel up the stairs to her bedroom.

She's the one that's dragging her feet, he realized. And with a punch of shock, he realized.

She's the one that could hurt me.

· ♥ · ♥ · ♥ · ♥ · ♥ ·

Why are you inviting him up to your room?

Rachel's mind was racing. Ren had caught her off guard, showing up to the bookstore unannounced. He was being friendly about it, and it was a nice gesture. But she knew what he was after.

The only problem was, she wasn't sure how she *felt* about what he was after.

Now, she was leading him up the three stories to her loft bedroom. At least Hailey and Cressida were downstairs. That would keep her from doing anything epically stupid, like sleeping with him.

Would it?

She winced, rubbing her face. It had better, she warned herself.

She needed some way to get control of this situation. He was saying the right things. He was appealing to that side of her that had always wanted him to apologize. And he looked better than she'd dreamed. He was saying he'd wait for her, that they could take it slow. He was bringing her food and volunteering to study with her.

He was considerate those years that you dated, too. It was why you fell in love with him. But when something more important came up...

She frowned. And that was the issue, wasn't it? He was always lovely – until he made a different choice.

She stepped into her bedroom, surveying it to make sure it wasn't too messy. Her dirty clothes were in the hamper, thankfully, and her bed was made.

He looked around, then glanced out the window. "This is nice," he said, taking in the view, then looking over her double bed, the maple dresser. "A little weird, though.

To be in your Grandma Frost's room." He grinned. "I remember thinking she'd kill me if she found out what we'd done together."

"Trust me, she considered it," Rachel said, shrugging. "But we wound up getting me birth control instead. After Mom had two unplanneds – me, and Hailey – Grandma got a lot more practical."

They were quiet for a long minute. Then Ren cleared his throat. "So, marketing strategy...?"

"That's not why you're here, and we both know it."

His dark eyes gleamed. "Well, I do want to help you, if I can," he said. "But no, it's not the main reason I'm here. I just want to spend some time with you."

She sat on the edge of the bed. He looked around.

"Sorry, three narrow flights of stairs are a long way to carry up furniture, so I don't have any chairs," she said, then patted the bed next to her. He sat down next to her, and she could feel the heat from his body. He still had his coat on.

She thought about taking it, but reducing the numbers of layers between them suddenly seemed like a bad idea.

Ren sighed. "Why don't you tell me what's worrying you, Rachel, and I'll see if I can address it?"

Putting it that way sounded so damned *logical.* "I'm scared of you, Ren."

"I told you, I'll give you as much time as you need to get used to me."

"That's part of the problem," Rachel said, then bounced up with nervous energy, pacing the room. "That sounds like… it feels like you're wearing me down by inches when you talk that way."

"You're a strong woman. You can say no at any time," Ren pointed out.

"By that point, it'll probably be too late," she muttered, and Ren shot her a grin. "I don't want to feed your ego, but you were always good at this stuff. You were a romantic. You were considerate and compassionate and generally speaking, a great boyfriend."

"Thank you," he said, sounding sincere.

"Which is why you blindsided me when you dumped me," she said.

He winced. "I don't see how else I can prove that I've changed than showing you through action, though." He got up, too, holding her, preventing her pacing. "Why don't you set a time limit?"

She blinked. "What are you talking about?"

"You don't want an open-ended courtship, apparently," he said, then grimaced. "Although 'courtship' sounds like something out of a Jane Austen novel. Anyway, you want to set some boundaries, feel more in control of the situation, am I right?"

She bit her lip. Damn it. He always could read her. She felt contrary, and crossed her arms. "Maybe," she said, even though they both knew she was lying.

"So why don't you set some ground rules? How long do I have to convince you, and what do I need to do?"

Her mind raced. That actually felt good. It gave her anxiety a focus and helped her feel like she was getting a grip on the situation.

"One week," she heard herself say, and drew herself up, standing straighter. "You've got one week to convince me."

Whatever he was expecting, it wasn't that. "One week? That's... that's barely any time at all!" he spluttered.

She felt relief come over her in a wave. "It's plenty of time," she countered. "Most people only need three dates or so to figure out if someone's worth spending more time with. Heck, most people only need *one* date."

"If that's the case," Ren countered, "then we're good to go. I'd say our first date went very well."

"After you answered your phone for work during it," she said.

He reddened. "That was rude," he admitted. "But it was a work emergency."

She held up a hand. "One week," she said, feeling more confident. "If you can get me over my reservations about you in one week, then I'll start dating you again."

"That seems really arbitrary," Ren complained.

"You were the one that said set a time limit," she replied.

"I was thinking more like six months. Or three months – you know, a business quarter." He looked at her with a sexy, imploring smile. "Dating with a quarterly performance review? You're a business woman, I would think that'd appeal to you."

He was thinking of how he could use it to his advantage, she thought. "One week," she repeated, more firmly.

He sighed, then nodded. "Okay. One week."

Her eyes widened. She was surprised he hadn't negotiated for more time.

"In that time," he said, with a lopsided smile, "I am going to romance the living *shit* out of you."

She burst out laughing. "Let's not go crazy."

"In exchange," he said, "I would like you to be available to being romanced. No dodging me for a week and then calling it off."

"I wouldn't do that," she scoffed. "I play fair."

"I know. Just putting some ground rules of my own down." He looked at her, his head tilting slightly. "So, it's a deal?"

She nodded. "It's a deal."

"Let's kiss on it."

Her breathing went shallow. "A handshake ought to do."

"I didn't get a kiss after our first date," he said. "And if we're going to do this, we might as well do it right, yeah?"

She swallowed hard. Then she shrugged. "I guess…"

Before she could finish her sentence, he moved in, his mouth covering hers, his lips pressing against her own.

His lips were firm, perfectly molding themselves to her. It was like getting into a warm bath, that feeling of perfect comfort and warmth.

Then, suddenly, things got hotter.

His mouth opened, his tongue teasing her lips until they parted, then moved in to sweep against her tongue. She felt the heat of it zing to her breasts and between her legs, and she reached up and grabbed his broad shoulders for some kind of stability as she felt the room give a lazy spin. He devoured her, and she found herself matching him, her mouth moving nimbly against his, her body pressing against him. He was hard against her – not just his muscles, but the jut of his erection.

You've got a bed right there, her body projected. *You know he'd be good.*

It was that little brainstorm that made her jerk away. "One other rule," she said. "Maybe we should keep sex out of the equation for the time being."

"Oh?" he croaked.

"Because I don't think straight when I... when we..."

He grinned. "Still?"

"If that kiss was any indication, yes," she said, noticing she was panting a little. *Shit*.

"But we can still kiss, right?" His eyes were puppy-dog cute and imploring, even as his grin was devilish.

"Yes," she said, then realized... kissing with him would probably lead to sex, if she wasn't careful. "Now, go on. I've got studying to do."

"I can still help."

"Not with that hard-on, you can't," she said, and he barked out a laugh. "I think that we'll only distract each other at this point. Go home, Ren."

"Okay," he said, and he brushed another kiss over her lips. "But be ready to go out tomorrow, okay?"

"All right," she said, then returned with a kiss of her own... which led to another kiss.

In moments, they were making out again, ravenously. Her hands went under his coat, tugging at his shirt. He had his hands woven in her hair, holding her tight to him. They finally pulled apart, breathless.

"You've got to go home," she said, shaking her head at herself. "I'll see you tomorrow."

He grinned, tucking his shirt back in. "Yes, ma'am. I'll see myself out." He winked. "Call you later?"

"Okay." She rubbed at her temples as he shut the door behind him.

Do you really think a week is going to save you?

She'd better start coming up with some safeguards, she realized. Because if tonight was any indication, she was sunk before she even had a chance.

CHAPTER 4

Ren stood at a whiteboard in one of the conference rooms. That morning's meeting had gone on a full hour longer than it should have, and now he was looking at the notes they'd taken for how to deal with the factory in Zhuhai, which was still having problems with productivity and process on the line. Next, he'd be dealing with the software problems they were having with the Electronics Division's sales functionality, and with the inventory system which directly linked up with the Zhuhai factory.

"You're going to need to talk to the software people tonight," Ted, one of his software engineers, said with a grimace.

"I'm not going to be in tonight," Ren said absently. "Do we have all the process notes right for these chips? It feels like we're missing a step somewhere."

"What do you mean, you're not going to be in tonight?"

Ren looked up at the sharp surprise in Ted's voice. "I've got to be out of the office by five-thirty," he said.

"Lessee... that'd be, what, nine-thirty in the morning in Zhuhai," Ted muttered. "Okay, you can still catch them in time, they'll be in by eight."

"I know," Ren said, feeling irritated. "Is that it, Ted?"

Ted didn't seem to register Ren's impatience. He grabbed his papers, then used his phone to take a picture of the whiteboard. "We'll have another check-in on Thursday."

Ren sighed. "What are we going to have to check in about in two days? Until we get the process stuff figured out and we iron out what we're going to do about the software developer, we're just going over the same ground, over and over."

"We can't make any decisions unless we go over every option, though," Ted said.

Ren frowned. "I'll set up a meeting with the COO and the CIO," he said.

Ted's eyes widened. "All right."

Ren grabbed his stuff and headed to his office. Work stuff had gotten steadily more challenging since his parents had moved him over to the troubled Electronics Division. He was currently working almost as a consultant, doing operations stuff. He knew it was a tough spot for the CIO to be in, as well: he was, essentially, acting as the boss of his boss's son. He knew that the guy felt threatened and a little resentful of Ren's position.

That said, Ren was also there to do a job. Things weren't working, and his parents had put him in place to make sure things *would* work. Whatever it took. Failure wasn't an option.

When is it ever an option?

When he got to his office, he saw his assistant, Stephen, in his adjoining smaller office. "Did you get everything set up for tonight?" he asked.

Stephen smiled. "Yup. Limo's going to pick her up and get her to the restaurant by six-thirty," he said. "You've got a private room with a view of the Ferris wheel and the pier. One of the best steakhouses in the city."

"And the gerbera daisies?" They were her favorite.

"They'll be waiting in the car."

Ren grinned back. *Romancing the shit out of her: achievement unlocked!*

"Now, I just need to come up with something for tomorrow," he muttered to himself, heading back into his office, only to have Stephen follow him.

"You've got some stuff to go over," Stephen said. "Jeremy from the software developer has called three times this morning, screaming about how it wasn't their fault the software's been buggy."

"They *designed* the software. If it isn't their fault, whose is it?" Ren asked, disgusted.

"They're saying it's user error."

"User error doesn't make the whole thing fail when it updates." Ren walked into his office, sitting at his desk.

"I'll give him a call. Do me a favor and pull our contract with them? I want to see what we can do to get out of that."

"Ren, can I speak with you a minute?"

Ren looked up. The division's Chief Operations Officer, Peter, was standing in the doorframe. He was a portly man with a receding hairline, his thin lips pulled in a tight line. "Yes, Peter?"

"It's about Zhuhai." Peter's pronunciation was atrocious.

"I'll pull that contract," Stephen said, then quickly exited the room, leaving them alone.

"I'm going to need you to go over there as soon as possible," Peter continued without preamble.

Ren bit back a sigh. Peter couldn't speak Mandarin or Cantonese, and they spoke both in Zhuhai. Sometimes Ren wondered if Peter didn't just see him as a high-level translator. "I think that it might be better if we get the process stuff straightened out first," Ren ventured. "There isn't much point in me being there if I can't get the line stuff figured out."

"So you'll see it firsthand."

"I think late February might be better," Ren said, gently but firmly. "Just a few more weeks."

Peter obviously disagreed, and Ren got the feeling he'd probably need to jump on a plane. "Well, I've got a meeting tonight at eight, with the factory head."

"That wasn't on my calendar," Ren said.

"It is now." Peter looked irritated. "We've obviously got to get this straightened out."

But I am getting it straightened out. Ren cleared his throat. "I can't tonight," he said. "I have a... an appointment."

Peter looked at him like he was insane. "So cancel it!"

Ren leveled a stare back at him. "I think it might be better if we reschedule this, so I have more time to go over the materials," he said.

Peter stared, and for a second, it was a game of chicken. Which one of them would blink first?

Peter's color was red by the time he sighed through gritted teeth. "*Fine*. We'll reschedule for tomorrow night."

Ren only had a week to romance Rachel. "Next week," he said.

Now Peter looked apoplectic. "It's going to take you a week to go through those materials?"

"Actually, it's going to take a few days to simply collect the materials," Ren pointed out, and he wasn't lying: they were still collecting information. "Then it's going to take a few days to make sure everyone who has to be there has the materials and goes over them prior to the meeting."

If Peter could've strangled him without repercussions, he probably would have. "Maybe we should discuss this with your father," he said, his voice rough.

Ren's eyes widened.

Seriously? You're going to bring my parents into this?

"I'd be happy to discuss it with him," Ren said. "In fact, I'll be sure to mention it this weekend, at brunch."

Peter blanched. Again, Ren felt badly: it had to suck to have your boss's kid working for you. But he was asking for things that were unrealistic, and Ren wasn't going to do stupid, pointless stuff just so his boss would feel better. Not if he didn't have to.

"Fine," Peter said. "Copy me on everything you send out." With that, he turned on his heel and walked away.

Ren rubbed at his forehead against a nascent headache. "Hey Stephen?"

Stephen popped his head in. "Yeah?"

"Make sure that you get me all the info that gets funneled in about the line process for the Zhuhai factory," he said. "And can you do me a favor?"

"Sure, what?"

"Keep my week – especially my evenings – clear for the next seven days." He frowned. "And if it's not too much trouble, I'm going to need to think of some really romantic dates."

Stephen looked at him like he'd grown another head. "Who *is* this woman, boss?"

Stephen had been his assistant for the past four years, following him from division to division. At this point, he was just as much a friend as a business associate, and Ren trusted him implicitly.

"She's special, and I'm trying desperately hard not to screw this up," he said. "I need to make sure I can spend time with her and not get buried under work, so just... run interference for me, okay? No bonehead stuff if we can avoid it."

Stephen nodded, looking resolute. "You got it, Ren."

Ren watched as Stephen left, then looked at the hundreds of emails he still had to go through in his in-box.

He thought of Rachel – her dark hair, those sparkling eyes, those full lips. The way she'd clung to him the night before. Those kisses...

You'll see her tonight, he chastised himself. Then he went back to work.

· ♥ · ♥ · ♥ · ♥ · ♥ ·

Rachel looked at herself critically in the mirror. Ren had told her to dress fancy tonight: he was sending a town car to pick her up, no doubt to take her to some ritzy restaurant or something. The problem was, she didn't really have a fancy wardrobe. The black dress she'd worn to the Seastar was probably the nicest dress she owned. She had plenty of nice work clothes, and she had a cocktail dress that she'd worn to a party the casino had last year, a royal blue satin number with lace. She was wearing that now, hoping that she wasn't overdressed. Or, God forbid, underdressed.

She could borrow something from Hailey, but Hailey had more of a figure than she had, and she was afraid that things would droop open. She looked at the cocktail dress critically. At least this fit.

She'd curled her hair a little, putting it in loose waves over her shoulders. She put on her makeup carefully.

Why can't I be the type that wraps a guy around her finger, then destroys him?

She looked great. She knew that she could be stunning, if she tried. If she were Hailey, she'd probably string Ren along for the whole week, then crush him under her big-heeled boot by the end of seven days. *Why can't I be like that?*

She was going to give him the full seven days, to see how compatible they were. He was going to "romance the shit out of her." And she knew he was charming and had the means.

Why even make the one week a thing? Why not just give in?

She watched her expression turn stubborn. Because he had hurt her, she thought. Because she might not be the Hourglass Amazon her sister was, but she wasn't going to let Ren run rampant over her, either.

There was a light knock on her door. "Rache? Can I come in?"

It was Cressida's gentle voice. "Sure," Rachel said. "Everything okay?"

Cressida stepped in. She was wearing a thick green sweater and a pair of khakis, as well as some thick socks that Hailey had gotten her for Christmas. "Ooh. You look amazing," Cressida said.

Rachel did a little spin, enjoying the way the shortish skirt spun out. "I have no idea where we're going, but I figure I'll be ready for anything in this."

Cressida sat on the bed, looking hesitant. Rachel sat next to her. "So, you're getting back together with him?" Cressida asked.

It wasn't in-your-face, like Hailey. Cressida's voice sounded tentative, wary.

Rachel sighed. "I don't know yet. I mean, in my head, part of me is saying make him work for it."

"He really hurt you." Cressida's expression was morose.

"I know." The pain was still there, though not as fresh as it had been. "He's apologized. That helped."

"But does he mean it?"

"You've been talking with Hailey about this, huh?" Rachel nudged Cressida, who nodded.

"Hailey's thinking more along the lines of a gun, a shovel, and quicklime," Cressida said, and Rachel let out a surprised laugh. "I'm just... worried."

"You don't need to be."

I know, it's not our business, but we love you," Cressida said earnestly. "And I'll back off after this."

"You're not pressuring me," Rachel assured her. "Believe me, you're not telling me anything I haven't thought of myself."

"He was never a bad guy," Cressida temporized. "What he did to you was bad, but he was an okay person."

"That's a ringing endorsement." Rachel shook her head. "He was a great guy. He just didn't prioritize me first." *Or second, or third,* she thought bitterly. "Right now, I'm in his radar. He wants me, so he's giving me the full court press. But what if something else comes up?"

That was what she was waiting for this week. For the other shoe to drop. For something to cross his path, something more important.

For him to drop her. *Again*.

She set her chin firmly, nodding. "So I'm not going to sleep with him. I'll let him wine me and dine me, and romance me. But we'll see if it goes any further."

She caught Cressida's smile. "That sounds like you're keeping your guard up, anyway."

"I'm trying."

She slipped on her shoes, a pair of high heels in a matching deep blue that she'd fallen in love with. Then the two of them headed down the stairs.

Hailey was there, ringing up a customer. She waited until the customer left, then looked around. Seeing that they had the store to themselves, Hailey turned to Rachel. "Are you *crazy*?"

"Hi, Hailey," Rachel said, tongue in cheek.

"What the hell are you doing? You let this guy come over to 'study' last night, and now you're going out to dinner with him? *Again*?"

Rachel reached for a thick black full-length wool coat. "Yes, Hailey. I am going out to dinner with him. Again."

"Are you just looking to get kicked like a puppy?"

"Hailey," Cressida reproached her. "You're not helping."

"I just want to know why my sister, who got kicked to the curb like *garbage* ten years ago, is suddenly all kissy-kissy with the guy who trashed her!"

Rachel stiffened. Hailey was the most demonstrative of the three of them, the most temperamental. She didn't suffer fools gladly.

Apparently, she believed Rachel was being a fool.

"He said he was sorry," she said. "I believe he meant it."

"Well of course he means it," Hailey said, rolling her eyes. "He wants you."

"We were lucky," Rachel said sharply, cutting across Hailey's protests. "Can you imagine what it would've been like if we *had* gotten married? Or stayed engaged?" She shook her head. "He would've been distracted at school, and so would I. I seriously doubt a long-distance relationship would've survived Grandma Frost's cancer. So yeah, he broke up with me, but at least it was a decent reason. I'm not going to pretend it didn't hurt, but I'm not going to let it keep dragging me down, either."

She stood up straighter, her spine stiffening as she slipped on her coat.

"The bottom line is: I'm a mature woman now. I know what I want – and *who* I want – and I know what I deserve.

I'm not going to just let him have me without working for it a little. And I'm damned well going to make sure that if – *if* – we get back together, he values me."

Hailey studied her, still looking a little suspicious. Then she nodded. "I just want to protect you," she said, her voice subdued. Especially for a Hailey tirade.

Rachel's heart melted a little. "I know. And I promise, I'll be careful."

"He always had a way of charming you out of being mad," Hailey said. "He comes from a rich family; he's used to getting his way. Don't let him walk over you."

"I won't."

There was suddenly a knock at the door. The sisters looked over. It was a place of business, so the knock was weird. Rachel walked over.

There was a man in a black suit with a snowy white shirt. "Car for, ah, Rachel Frost?" he said, then gave her a quick look. His eyes filled with admiration. "You're Rachel Frost?"

She nodded.

He gestured to the gleaming black limo. "I'm taking you to the city," he said. "Traffic's gonna be a bit of a challenge, but if you're ready to go…"

She grabbed her purse, then impulsively hugged Hailey and Rachel. Then she took a deep breath, turning back to the driver.

"I'm ready," she said, even as her stomach knotted. At least, she was as ready as she was going to get.

· ❤ · ❤ · ❤ · ❤ · ❤ ·

Ren was waiting by the hostess' station at the steakhouse when Rachel arrived. His eyes roamed over her black coat, then widened appreciatively when she unbuttoned it, revealing the royal blue dress beneath. She looked gorgeous, the blue bringing out the deep royal tones of her eyes.

"You look stunning," he said, leaning in and kissing her cheek as she hugged him.

She slung her coat over her arm. "Thanks," she said. The cold air had pinkened her cheeks and brightened her eyes. "This is a nice place."

"I hope you like it," he said, then turned to the hostess, who was smiling at the two of them.

"If you'll just follow Phillip, here?" the hostess said, gesturing to a waiter who was standing at attention like he was in the military. He gestured, then led the way to a private room that had a huge floor-to-ceiling set of windows, with a gorgeous view of the city beyond. Ren was gratified when he heard Rachel's gasp of pleasure.

"You like?" he asked.

"It's amazing!" she marveled, standing closer to the windows.

"May I take your coat, miss?" Phillip asked. Silently, distracted, she handed it over. He hung it on a nearby coat rack. The room itself was paneled in dark woods, with a sideboard. The single table was covered in snowy white linen, with emerald green napkins.

Rachel turned, then noticed Phillip had pulled her chair out. Her cheeks went a little darker as she sat on the seat, letting Phillip push her in. Ren sat across from her.

"Would you like to see the wine list?"

"I'm not a big wine drinker," Rachel protested.

"We have a variety of mixed drinks," Phillip said.

"How about a Kir Royale?" Ren suggested. "It's got black current liqueur and champagne. You always liked champagne."

"That does sound good," Rachel said, turning to Phillip. "Thanks."

Phillip handed them their menus. "I will be back shortly to discuss specials and help you with absolutely anything you require," he said, sounding like it would be his genuine pleasure to run out in traffic if they asked him to. Ren shook his head.

"We'll be ready in a minute."

Phillip left them alone. Both Rachel and Ren were sitting on one side of the table, looking out at the view beyond.

"This is really great, Ren," Rachel said, sounding overwhelmed.

"I told you: gonna romance the hell out of you," he joked, taking her hand. She didn't pull away, to his relief.

He stroked the soft skin at the back of her hand before turning it over, stroking her palm. "How was today?"

"Uneventful. Better now," she said, and he felt his body tighten.

"I know how you feel," Ren said, his voice roughening. "I know my day got a whole lot better as soon as you walked through the door of the restaurant."

I haven't been able to stop thinking about those kisses. He'd been impatient all through the work day, getting progressively more irritated with the petty distractions that apparently only he could deal with.

But he wasn't going to unload all of that on her. He was romancing her, not dumping on her.

"Do you take a lot of people here?" she asked, looking at him from under full black lashes.

He blinked, surprised at the turn of the conversation. "Do you mean, do I date a lot? Or do I go through this much trouble?"

"Either." Rachel smiled. "Both."

"The answer: I don't date much. Like you, I don't have a whole lot of time." Although he was deliberately making time this week, he realized. "When I do date, I don't tend to get a private dining room, no."

"I just figured this was the way that billionaires ate and entertained." She drawled. "A girl could get used to this. What were you planning on doing to top this tomorrow night?"

He actually sat back, releasing her hand. He'd wanted to impress her, sure. But her voice sounded so... so mercenary.

Had she changed?

She shot him a quick grin, and he realized abruptly that he'd been taken in.

"I know you want to 'romance the shit out of me', but did you really think that you had to pull a Christian Grey to do it?" she said gently. "Expensive food and exclusive restaurants?"

"Well, it does head towards a red room of pain," he quipped, deadpan, "so I figured the lead up at least ought to be good."

Her laugh was intoxicating. "You had money when we were dating, in high school," she said. "But that wasn't why I was with you, and you know it. We went out for burgers all the time. I didn't expect, or want, jewelry or gifts or any of that."

He felt his cheeks heat. "Apparently this is a miss?"

"No," she said, and to his relief, *she* took *his* hand. "What I'm saying is, you don't need to spend a ton of money to impress me. If I'm going to stay together with you, your ability to take me out to fancy restaurants and throw gobs of money at me aren't going to be the reason why."

He swallowed, a lump forming in his throat. He felt... humbled.

"In fact," she said, her voice mischievous, "I'd like to make a rule. For the rest of the week, you don't get to spend more than fifty dollars on a date with me."

He frowned, doing the math. "Per person?"

"Total."

"*Total?*" he croaked. "Which leaves me with exactly *where* to take you?"

"Maybe you don't have to take me out to dinner," she said. "Maybe we could grab burgers one night, or go to a movie. Or maybe you could cook for me."

He thought about it. Cooking for her – that could get her over to his place. Of course, she had the no-sex rule in place already, so that could be torturous.

"I'll work with it," he agreed, squeezing her hand. Her answering smile told him that it would be difficult, but God willing, it would be worth it.

CHAPTER 5

After their luxurious dinner and dessert, Rachel felt cozy and pampered. They went back down to the waiting driver and the limo.

"I wanted to hang out, spend some time with you in the back," Ren said, with a small smile. "It'll be at least a half an hour, probably more in this weather. That's time we could spend together."

The partition was up, and she smirked at him. "Is that what you tell all the girls?"

"Never before," he said, then patted the seat next to him. "C'mon. I was just thinking a little snuggling. We can still take it slow."

She worried at the corner of her lip with her teeth. He did things to her self-control. Of course, she was already this far…

What the hell.

She snuggled up against his side, breathing in his spicy cologne, and the car pulled out into Seattle traffic. She felt him tilt his head, nuzzling her.

"God, you feel good," he breathed, and he sounded grateful. "Have I mentioned recently how glad I am that you're seeing me again?"

"Jury's still out," she said, even though she felt more and more attracted to him. It felt like putting up a battle was more and more futile.

"I mean just seeing me for dinner and things." And he really did sound happy about it. He stroked her arm, fitting her tight against his side. "And talking to you on the phone. And... I don't know. Just being with you."

She felt her chest warm, and it had nothing to do with the heating controls in the limo. "It's weird. It's been a while since I've been with anyone but my girlfriends, or my sisters." She smiled. "I still hang out with the same girls from high school, can you believe it?"

"Really?" He pulled back to look at her. "Stacy?"

"And Hailey's friend Kyla, and Mallory," Rachel reminded him. "We all hang out at least monthly at the bookstore. Girls' night, although almost everyone's paired off now." She frowned, realizing that.

Almost everyone I know is in a relationship.

That didn't mean she had to be. She wondered absently if she was reacting to Ren because of loneliness, on top of all the other baggage she had about him.

She felt him brush his mouth against her hair, and then against the curve of her ear. "It's great that you've stayed in contact," he said. She shivered at the sensual feel of his breath against her earlobe, and the sensitive skin behind it, near her neck.

"Y-yes. They're the best." What was she talking about? She felt a small moan emerge, and she squelched it as best she could. His lips brushed lower, sucking gently. He pressed a kiss at the little hinge of her jaw, on her now wildly pounding pulse.

"I wonder..." he started, then cursed softly when his phone went off. "Sorry. I meant to shut it off, but there have been some work crises lately. I told my brother I'd keep it on."

"It's okay." And it really was. She was being drawn into his spell, like hypnosis. She needed a little distance. "I mean..."

He went straight for her, his mouth brushing against hers, but gently, like a butterfly. She gasped. That went on for some time. It was like he was exploring a strange new world, even though they'd spent a lot of their formative years learning to kiss from each other.

She loved the feel of him. The taste of him.

Oh, why keep fighting it?

She closed her eyes, then leaned forward, returning the kiss with one of her own. It was tentative. The last thing she wanted to do was tear off her clothes in the back of this limo and ravish him.

Is it, though? Is it really the last thing you want to do?

Well, she thought to herself. It was still on the list, apparently.

Ren wove his fingers into her hair, keeping her in place as his mouth carefully and thoroughly devoured hers. His tongue moved forward, stroking against hers gently, lovingly. She made an aching sigh that his mouth captured, and her hands clenched his shoulders, holding him tight.

She wasn't sure when he'd undone the buttons on her coat, but she quickly shucked it off and tore at his jacket, shoving it off of his shoulders.

Keep your clothes on!

She groaned a little. She wanted to rebel against that, *so badly*.

He was pressed against her, and he twisted her until they were face to face. She moved, straddling him, her skirt billowing over his knees. She moved until she could feel his hardness, notching into the junction of her thighs, and she tilted her head back.

"*Ren*," she said sharply, moving her hips, and she was gratified when he groaned with her, his hips lifting, his hands smoothing down the lacy panels over her breasts, down to her hips, holding her even tighter against his cock.

"Oh, God, Rachel," Ren said, through gritted teeth. His hips jolted up, and she felt herself going slick, her clit a hard little bead.

She'd forgotten how much she missed this. Not from just any man – she could have sex with other men if she wanted – but with *Ren.* The way he'd made her feel special. The way he'd simply wanted her, like no other man had ever...

Buzzzzzzzz.

She frowned. Was that his phone? Again?

After a few minutes, it stopped. Then started up again.

He pulled away, breathless, his eyes angry. "I am *so* sorry," he said, then looked at his phone, glaring at it before answering. "What the *hell*, Jian?"

She shifted off his lap, already feeling the absence of his erection with a definite pang of disappointment. But she wasn't going to stay on his lap while he took a business call, or family call, or whatever the hell this was. It had to be some kind of emergency, like he said.

Ren's eyes narrowed. "He called the meeting without me? I told him I had plans tonight!" He sounded angry. "And he called Mom and Dad? *Fucker*."

Rachel sighed. Well, it was a business emergency, apparently. She was glad it wasn't a medical emergency or something like that, but – well, she'd been getting pretty close. It might not have taken too much more rubbing to get her there, she realized.

Not that it was a good idea, if she was trying to keep some distance. But it wouldn't be *sex*, per se.

You are so making this shit up as you go along.

CATHY YARDLEY

She grinned at herself, and at her excuses. She still wanted Ren, she had no doubts about that. She just wasn't sure if her heart could take him.

He kept on talking, something about meetings and a factory and software stuff. Then she heard him say: "Fine. I'll be back tonight and talk to them then."

She blinked. It was already nearly ten.

He hung up, then turned back to her. He looked tired, and irritated. "Sorry. Where were we?"

"We've stopped," she realized.

They looked out the window. Between their make-out session and Ren's phone call, and the driver's skill, it had only taken them half an hour to get to her house. Now, the bookstore loomed at the top of the walk.

She turned to him. "So – I guess a nightcap is out of the question?" she asked, knowing if she got him into her bedroom, she'd probably make some bad decisions that wouldn't let him leave until morning.

He must've read the intent on her face, because he looked truly regretful. "I can't," he said, with a low, soft curse. "I have to go back into the office."

She tilted her head, considering that.

He's saying no to you, so he can go back to work.

Her eyes narrowed.

I'm going to be too busy for you...

Red flag, she thought. Huge, serious red flag.

"But I'll see you tomorrow," he said. "I don't have the place set up, since you just instituted the whole fifty-dollar cap, but..."

"It's not a big deal," she said. "I've got my test tomorrow, anyway."

He frowned. "Let my driver take you," he said. "It's supposed to snow tomorrow, and the roads are going to be a mess."

She shook her head. "I was taking care of myself for years before you were here, with your fancy dinner and limos and drivers," she said, with a little laugh. "I can manage driving myself to school, thanks."

He huffed. "I'm really sorry I have to go."

She leaned forward, kissing him lingeringly, until she felt him reach for her. Then she pulled away.

"It's probably just as well," she said. "I might've broken my no-sex rule, and then where would we be?"

The look on his face was priceless. She was chuckling to herself all the way up the stairs to the house. But as she closed the door behind her, she realized: she was right. She was falling for him, *again*. And it sounded like his job made college look like a picnic.

He's going to hurt you, she told herself.

And like any good train wreck, she couldn't seem to look away.

· ♥ · ♥ · ♥ · ♥ · ♥ ·

Ren fumed all the way back to the city, all the way back to Chu corporate headquarters. He waved to the security guard as he stalked through the empty hallways. It was *ten-fucking-thirty* at night, for pity's sake. Why was he here?

Because the Chief Operating Officer has a bug up his ass.

He hit the elevator button, then ascended all the way to the thirtieth floor. He headed out. The cleaning crew was there, vacuuming and emptying trash cans. "Hey, Ren," one of the custodians, Paul, said with a nod.

Ren nodded back. "Have a good holiday?"

"Great one," he said, then gave Ren a glance. "Back to working late again, huh?"

Ren sighed. "Looks like it."

"Well, don't work too hard." Paul's laugh was rasping.

Ren smiled back as best he could. He didn't feel like laughing. He felt like strangling somebody.

He closed his eyes for a second, Rachel's familiar scent filling his nostrils, the feel of her satiny dress under his fingertips. His body tensed momentarily, as he thought of her, spreading over him, swaying against him...

No. He growled at himself silently. No time for that kind of indulgence.

He was here to kick some ass.

He headed for Peter's office, saw the light was on. He headed inside, knocking on the doorframe. "Peter, I..."

He stopped abruptly, taking in the other people in Peter's office.

"Hello, Ren," Ren's mother said, her smile small and calm. No matter what hour of day or night, she always looked impeccably dressed and ready for a photo shoot. She was wearing what looked like a Chanel suit tonight. She got to her feet, giving him a small hug and pressing her cheek against his.

His father was sitting in another chair and nodded to him curtly. He was broad-chested, wearing a similarly impeccable suit. No off-the-rack for his father, not even couture. Everything was privately made by his personal tailor in Hong Kong.

"I knew he'd called you, but I didn't think you'd both be here this late," Ren said.

"It's the family business," his father said, sounding surprised at Ren's surprise – and reproachful. "Of course we came right away."

Ren couldn't stop himself from glaring at Peter.

"What really surprised me," his father continued, "was that you weren't here. That you knew there was a meeting, but you *refused* to be here."

So that's how Peter was spinning it, huh? Ren shook his head. "I didn't need to be here. Honestly, Dad, neither do you."

"That's not how I see it," Peter said, his smile catlike and smug. "I told you there were issues that needed to be addressed with the factory, and you told me you wouldn't be able to deal with it for a *week*. That's hardly the kind of assertive, problem-solving approach we use here at Chu."

He sounded like a kiss-up. He *was* being a kiss-up... and he was trying to discredit Ren in front of his own family.

"The factory is going to need work, no question. But that's going to be a matter of both process and hiring," Ren said. "Which we're not going to get nailed down tonight. We're not solving anything in the next twenty-four hours. We don't even have key people in place, with the information they need, to start making the decisions that would solve the problems."

Ren's father pinched his mouth a little. "Peter mentioned that you were out with a girl tonight, instead of dealing with the factory. Is that true? And that you've cleared the rest of the week to be available to her?"

Ren winced. So *Peter* had known about that, huh? He'd have some fucking words with Stephen about that little tidbit, as well.

"I did have a date tonight, yes," he said. "I am hoping to see her more, not just this week. Not that it's any of Peter's business."

Peter's grin widened a fraction.

"Of course, Peter, I told you this afternoon that I'd talk to my parents about everything that was going on. I told you that the meeting ought to be rescheduled until everyone who needed to had the information that they needed actually *got it*. But instead, you run around like a chicken with its head cut off, acting busy just so you can justify your job, putting in a late night so you think you can look good. Tell me: what did the discussion with the Zhuhai factory lead come up with tonight?"

Peter's complexion turned ruddy with anger as Ren's parents turned to him.

"We've got some promising ideas," he said, his voice tight.

"Really? Can you name one? Just one."

"The... the... uh..." He cleared his throat. "We were talking about replacing the head engineer."

"We talked about that two weeks ago. It's in my email of recommendations that I made to you then. It might still be in your inbox," Ren added uncharitably. "Anything else of value come out of tonight's late-night session? Because I've been in the office since seven this morning, and I knew that there wouldn't be any point to staying until eight or later tonight, just to have a meeting that nobody was ready for!"

Ren knew that his voice had raised. His mother looked at him, her eyebrows arching. She didn't like being demonstratively angry. It was what made her such a fierce businesswoman. She was brilliant, and often underestimated.

His father was nodding. "Well, it does feel like you've got your arms wrapped around this problem," he said to Ren, then looked at Peter. "I'm sorry that you feel like Ren isn't taking this seriously enough, but I assure you, nobody takes our business more seriously than our family."

It was a rebuke, but a subtle one. Given the need, the Chu family would stand behind their own. Peter must've put that together, as well, because his reddened complexion turned a pale white.

"I just thought you should know," Peter said. "I'll be in early tomorrow, and we'll get these problems ironed out."

"I feel certain you will," Ren's mother said, and her tone, though even, brooked no argument. "We promised stockholders that the problems would be addressed by this year."

Which put a ticking clock on the time bomb that was the Electronics Division. Ren saw Peter swallow hard, then nod.

"Come on, walk us out," his mother said, looping her arm through his and walking with him out of Peter's office. "I want to hear about this date. Anyone we know?"

"No, Mom." He winced. *Goddamn Stephen*. What was he thinking, letting that detail slip?

"Good family?" By his mother's definition, a "good family" was one that was nearly as wealthy as theirs, or at least one with serious business and/or social connections.

"I think so," he dodged, and her little mouth pursed as she read between the lines.

"You *are* taking this seriously, aren't you?" his father said, flanking him on the other side. "Peter can be an ass, you and I both know that, and he's on thin ice so he's getting desperate. But the bottom line is, you weren't here when the software went down the other day, either. Jian told me. You were on a date, then, weren't you?"

"Yes."

"Same girl?"

He thought of Rachel. Beautiful, sensuous, wonderful Rachel. Her laugh, her smile.

He sighed.

"Yes," he admitted.

His father looked disgruntled. "Now is not the time to get distracted," he warned Ren.

"When is?"

"Don't be a smartass," his father barked. "We moved you to the Electronics Division because it needs help. You know that. If that means you sleep in the office, you goddamned *sleep in the office*."

"We have made promises," his mother added, her voice firm.

"You went to all those internships, you've done work in all the other divisions, preparing you for just this kind of challenge," his father said. "Someday, you'll be taking over for me as head of the corporation. If you can't handle this, what makes you think you can take the reins when you're overseeing the entire corporation?"

Ren grimaced. "I've trained my whole life for this," he quipped.

"Yes, you did," his father said, and Ren winced. *Rachel would've gotten the reference*, he thought. And abruptly, overwhelmingly missed her.

"We know you can handle this," his mother said, then added, "as long as you're able to stay focused. As long as you don't let distractions get in the way."

Read: as long as you don't let a woman throw you off.

"Your social life needs to fit around your work, not the other way around," his father reminded him.

What social life?

"I will make sure my work gets done," Ren said. "My social life won't interfere."

His father nodded, satisfied. His mother, on the other hand, seemed to notice his wordplay, and her eyes narrowed.

"Maybe we should meet this girl," she murmured.

"It's too soon," Ren quickly said. They had found out that he'd proposed to Rachel, but not until they'd been engaged for a year – the summer before he'd gone off to college. The pressure to break up with her had been enormous. They'd guilt tripped. They'd pointed out the distance, the time. How he owed them to focus on his studies. And they'd strongly hinted that, were he to continue in this ill-fated relationship, they would cut him off: no financial support, no contact with family. In the end, he'd given in, knowing that it was probably for the best.

At least, it had seemed like it at the time.

Now, he wasn't sure how they'd react if they realized he was seeing Rachel again.

"We'll be checking in," his father said finally, as they made it to their respective cars. "So you'd better make some progress."

Ren thought of Rachel. He wanted to make progress there, too.

The only problem was – how the hell was he supposed to do that *and* be in the office for twelve plus hours a day?

· ♥ · ♥ · ♥ · ♥ · ♥ ·

"Rachel! How'd you think you did?" A fellow student, Tommy, came jogging up to her after the quiz. "If that was a quiz, I'm going to hate to see what his tests look like."

Rachel smiled. Tommy was like a puppy, sort of bouncing all over the place. "I think I did okay," she demurred. Actually, she thought she aced it. But she knew Tommy was struggling, and she didn't want to rub it in.

They headed down the long hallway towards the outer doors. "Hey, a few of us are going to go grab burgers," Tommy said. "You want to come with?"

She suppressed a sigh. Tommy was a kid. Not that she had any problems with age differences, generally speaking, but she was twenty-eight, and Tommy was twenty-three and often acted eighteen on a good day. They could engage in some great geek talks, but he'd horse around with some of the other young guys in the class, or talk about going to parties on campus. She shook her head. Really, an MBA guy at a frat party? She just knew that she didn't want any part of that.

"Who else is coming?" she asked carefully.

His grin widened. "I don't know. We'll find out when we get there." He tried for a look of innocence.

Which was his way of trying to ask her out under the guise of "everybody's going." Now she sighed aloud.

"Sorry, Tommy, I have plans tonight," she said, and they stepped outside. Snow was falling in fat, plush flakes. She felt the cold like little flashes as each flake hit her cheeks. "Oh, damn it."

She loved snow. It was beautiful, making the world pristine and quiet. The problem was, Seattle was many things, but designed for snow? With its narrow streets and steep hills, not so much. Fortunately, they didn't get snow that often. But when they did... gah.

"Oh, man. You live out in the boonies, right?" Tommy said. "It looks like it's really coming down."

"I see that." She wrapped her scarf around her throat and pulled on her hat. "Well, tonight's drive is going to be fun."

"You might want to think about staying in the city."

She laughed. "I'm not renting a hotel room just to avoid some snow."

"You could stay with me," he said, with a wink.

"Tommy," she warned.

"Hey. You can't blame a guy for trying." He sounded cheerful. "See you at class next week?"

"Yeah." She watched as he galumphed off, quickly chatting up another student, a younger woman named Mathilde who seemed far more eager for his attention. Good for them, Rachel thought. Guys that young were exhausting.

She pulled out her phone. Ren had texted her that he'd be working late, but that he'd come get her when her test was done. With the weather turning the way it was, all she wanted to do was get home where it was warm and cozy. She pulled out her phone and called him.

"Hey there," he said, his voice rumbly and low. "How'd it go?"

"Can't be positive, but I feel confident I nailed it," she said, smiling.

"That's great." He sounded so encouraging. She just wanted to cuddle up with that voice. "So now what? It's only eight. We could..."

"I was calling because I wanted to cancel tonight," she interrupted.

He sighed. "Oh?"

"It's snowing here, and the drive back is going to be a mess," she said quickly. "I don't want to think about hanging out here for another few hours, letting the snow pile up, then having to crawl across the bridge and down I-90 to get back home in the slush and the snow."

"That does sound dangerous." He paused. "You know, you could... okay. Let me preface this with: I am not making a pass at you."

She laughed. "Oh-kay."

"But you could stay here. With me. In the city," he clarified. "That way, you won't have to drive home in the weather and the dark."

Unlike Tommy's flirtatious offer, this felt like genuine concern. "I can handle it," she said.

"I'm not doubting your driving abilities," he countered. "I'm just saying: it sucks out tonight. If you can avoid it, maybe you should."

"I'll still have to go to work in the morning," she pointed out, then shut her mouth with an audible click. *Am I really considering this?*

"By then, they'll have plowed," he said, his voice smooth and persuasive. "And if you go in the morning, at least there'll be some light."

She bit her lip, considering it.

"No," she finally drew out.

"Okay," he said, backing off. "Mind if I ask why, though?"

Her mind flashed back to the limo... grasping hands, the way their mouths fused together. "You know why," she said, her voice low and raspy.

"I promise I'll be a complete gentleman."

"Oh?"

"Well," he said, "a PG-13 gentleman, at the very least. I do still want to convince you that dating is a good idea, and hopefully a little making out is involved."

She chuckled. At least he was being honest. "Would you consider going to a frat party?" she asked.

There was silence on the line. "Do you *want* to go to a frat party?"

"God, no." She laughed.

"I didn't go to frat parties when I was in college," he said. "Not that there's anything wrong with them, I suppose, I just didn't have the time or the bandwidth for parties and that kind of thing. My family would've killed me."

That sobered her.

I'm going to be too busy for you, Rachel.

"Well, I'm going to head out," she said, as she got to her car.

"I get another day."

She blinked. "Huh?"

"You said you'd figure it out in a week," he said. "I get another day of courting you to help you make that decision, if you're canceling on me tonight."

She smirked. "Do you really think another twenty-four hours is going to make a difference?"

"I'll take any advantage I can get." He let out a low sigh of disappointment. "Just... please be careful. And call me when you get home?"

"Okay," she said, with an eye roll.

"Not just to let me know you're okay. So we can talk."

She felt her belly knot, warming at that. She liked talking with him, as well.

Especially in bed.

"I'll talk to you in a bit," she said, then hung up. She climbed into her cold car, hoping that her heater would decide to work full blast. She turned her key.

Nothing.

She frowned. "Oh, come on, baby. Don't do this to me. Not now." She turned the key in the ignition again.

The engine made a sickly sound, like a cow being tipped. Then nothing.

"Oh, no, no, no..."

She got out, debating opening the engine. Hailey would know what to do... but then, Rachel wasn't Hailey. She felt tears of frustration fill her eyes.

Here she was, in a cold parking lot at the University of Washington, at eight o'clock at night, in a full snow storm. With a dead car.

Fantastic.

She took a deep breath. She could probably call roadside assistance, but by the time they got out there, she'd be dragging the car to some car repair place. And she really only trusted her friend Kyla with her car – she winced at the tow truck price to bring her car all the way back to Snoqualmie. In the meantime, she'd be out in the cold for half an hour *waiting* for the tow truck, at the very least. She'd bet there were plenty of accidents tonight, from the snow and ice.

Damn it!

She pulled her phone out of her pocket. Ren's place would be warm, she thought. And he was nearby, relatively speaking.

She opened up her contacts, then selected him, hitting dial and closing her eyes.

"That was fast," he said.

"My car won't start."

"Where are you?" he said immediately. "I'll come pick you up."

She took a deep breath. "All right." She told him the building and the lot number.

"We'll take care of your car and everything tomorrow, don't worry," he reassured her. "I'll be there as soon as I can."

He hung up, and she shivered in her car. So she was going to stay at Ren's house.

She was going into the lion's den.

He promised to be a perfect, PG-13 gentleman.

The only problem was, she hadn't promised anything.

CHAPTER 6

It was around eight-thirty when Ren finally got Rachel back to his condo. She was shivering in her car when he'd picked her up, but now she was warm, and hopefully she'd be comfortable at his place. He found himself a little anxious when he opened the door, ushering her inside.

"Wow," she said. "This is nice."

"It's not too much, is it?" he asked. "I just use it as a place to sleep, really. I bought it, but my Mom sent in her interior designer."

"It definitely looks all pulled together."

Was that a good thing, or a bad thing? He glanced around. Everything was sort of modern and minimalist and tasteful, in muted shades of gray and slate blue and sage green and silver. It was funny how he'd barely noticed it before.

He heard Rachel's stomach growl. "When was the last time you ate?"

"Lunch," she admitted. "With the test and all, I didn't really have time for dinner."

"Well, I said I'd feed you, and I think going out or waiting for takeout is going to be a mess," he said. "It's not fancy, but how about my fallback food?"

"What's that?" she asked with a grin, taking off her coat.

"Grilled cheese and tomato soup."

"A staple, and a classic," she said, her eyes darting around for someplace to stow her coat and backpack. He took both, gesturing for her to follow him. He led her to the guest bedroom, turning on the light. This room was done in shades of gold and wheat, with a sumptuous sheen over everything.

"This is your room," he said.

"Very nice," she said, with clear admiration. "You know, someone else offered to let me stay over at his place tonight, but I get the feeling he didn't have a spare bed in mind."

Ren felt jealous like a hot, vicious punch. "Oh?" he asked, keeping his voice calm. Or at least, he hoped he did.

She laughed, and he guessed he didn't do as well as he'd hoped. "It was this kid from school. He's the one that still goes to frat parties. He's been trying to ask me out for a year."

"Is he having some trouble taking no for an answer?" Ren said, his voice low and intense.

"Why? Would you engage in fisticuffs over me?" she said with a mock British accent, shaking her head.

"I take MMA lessons to keep in shape, and to blow off steam," Ren said. Which reminded him: he hadn't had a chance to get in the ring all last week, thanks to the Zhuhai shenanigans. "If the guy's bothering you, I can make him stop, believe me."

Rachel's eyes widened. "You're serious," she said. "Huh."

He couldn't help it. He reached out, stroked her cheek. "I don't want anyone harassing you, or hurting you," he said.

They stared at each other for a long minute. Then she seemed to shake herself off, her smile weak. "Well, I appreciate it, but I can take care of myself," she said. "And you know if anybody tried anything, Hailey would have probably maimed them with a tire iron."

"She's formidable," he agreed. "C'mon. Let's get you fed."

She followed him back to the kitchen, cooing over his stainless steel appliances and the size of his fridge. He felt oddly proud that she liked it. Maybe she'd be able to start envisioning herself here, he thought.

Wait, whoa. Living together?

He'd only reconnected with her a month ago, only started regularly talking to her a few days ago. But in his gut, he knew. He'd screwed up, letting her go. She was still funny, still fun – still smart, and thoughtful, and strong. Beyond that, there were things that he still wanted to learn about her, mysteries that he was still learning. He got the feeling he'd be able to learn more about her for years, and he was looking forward to it.

If she lets me.

He got out two cast iron pans and heated them on the iron burners as he got out a loaf of sourdough, putting out slices and loading them up with mustard, black pepper, and grated cheddar cheese. He put the tomato soup in bowls, having Rachel microwave them. Then he brushed the sandwiches with a bit of melted butter and popped them between the pans, letting the heat melt the cheese and toast the bread. In a few minutes, they were at his dining table, chowing down.

"This is *so* good," she murmured around a mouthful. "Oh, my God."

"I'm a late night snacker," he said, his chest puffing out a bit. "I sometimes work long hours. This was my go-to snack in college."

"I can see why." She swallowed hard. "Can I ask you a question?"

"Of course." He crunched into his sandwich.

She looked hesitant, her violet eyes clearly tentative. "Did you miss me? When you went off to college?"

He swallowed hard, the sandwich jagged in his throat. "Of course I did." At the time, he'd been homesick, studying his ass off, and missing her like a lost limb.

"How long before you had another girlfriend?"

"It was a while," he said. "I didn't date anybody freshman year. Not the first semester of sophomore year, either."

"Oh." She shrugged. "Not that it matters, really. I just always wondered."

"Wondered what?"

"How long it took to get over me, I guess." Her laugh was rough. "That's stupid."

"No," he said. Then he frowned. "How long before you... you know? Started seeing someone else?"

"I didn't have a boyfriend until senior year of college." She grimaced. "But I did sleep with several guys, starting in freshman year. Mostly in an attempt to forget you."

He winced. He couldn't blame her, but he suddenly wanted to see each and every one of those men in the ring, so he could beat their brains out.

Dude, get a grip.

"Like I said before, I've had a few relationships that didn't work out, and now I'm focusing on my school, my work, my family." Where she'd sounded matter-of-fact about it before, she now sounded a little forlorn. "You must understand that. It's not like a relationship fits easily into that dynamic."

"Not easily," he agreed. "But it's not impossible, either."

Her lips quirked on either side. "Says the single man who went back into work at ten o'clock last night."

"Touché." He nodded to concede her point. "Let's just say I *believe* that it's possible to have a relationship and do all that other stuff."

"I don't." Her words fell like a stone between them. "Not without prioritization, anyway. And some really hard boundaries. You can't give everything to everybody, you'd just disappear, get crushed under the weight of everyone's expectations."

"That's true." He frowned. "You're juggling three things. How do you manage?"

"My sisters are supportive," she said. "They run the store, and know that I can only work on weekends, and that's mostly the books and administrative stuff, which Cressida helps with. The casino knows that I'm working on my MBA, and my grad program knows that I'm working with a job. I negotiate what I need, when I need it."

He nodded. "So, what do you need from me?" he asked, in a low voice.

"Who says I need anything from you?"

He stayed serious, ignoring her attempt at playfulness. "What do you *want* from me, then?"

She sighed. "I want to know where I stand with you. I want assurances that you're not going to hurt me."

I'm still in love with you.

It was too early, way too early, and way too stupid to make that kind of a declaration now, so he bit back on it. "I am not going to hurt you."

"You're not going to want to," she said, getting up and grabbing the now empty plates and bowls. "But at some point, you're going to have a hard choice, and I am not sure that I'm going to be on the plus side of that decision matrix, you know?"

He wanted to say that it was unfair. He'd made the wrong choice ten years before, when he was eighteen. "I will always put you first," he said instead, his voice solemn.

"Don't." Her eyes flashed. "Don't say shit like that. You can't possibly mean it, and it makes me distrust you."

"How am I supposed to convince you?" He said, his own voice raising a little. "I said I'd go slow. You didn't like the idea of losing control. So I gave you control – and you gave me a week to convince you that I was a worthwhile bet. It's not fair, Rachel."

She seemed to crumple in on herself a little. "I know," she said. "I don't want to give you fair right now. It's a little lowering to find that, after all this time, I'm still hurting. And I'm still angry as hell at you."

He sighed. As unhappy as he was about it, he wasn't about to tell her that her feelings weren't valid.

"I'll just hope you can forgive me, then," he said. He cleared the plates and bowls, putting them in the dishwasher. "I really am sorry, Rachel."

"I know," she said. "I'm just... I'm scared."

He held her, hugging her tight against him. He would do anything to help her feel better – to feel more secure in him. In *them*.

But all he could do was wait on her, and hope that, unlike him, she would make the right decision when it came to their relationship.

· ♥ · ♥ · ♥ · ♥ · ♥ ·

It was midnight, and Rachel still wasn't asleep. The guest bedroom was great, so it wasn't that. There were blackout curtains, and the bed was memory foam, with just the right amount of give. She tossed and turned. She'd watched TV with Ren until eleven, and then had decided to turn in. She was wearing one of his T-shirts and a pair of sweatpants as pajamas, since she obviously hadn't been prepared to spend the night anywhere prior to her car debacle.

"Make yourself at home," he'd said, before they'd turned in for the night.

She felt hot. He kept the thermostat higher than they did at home, she figured. She also felt parched. What she really needed was a glass of water, and then she could slip off the sweatpants, and sleep more comfortably.

Hell. Maybe she'd slip off *everything*.

She thought about the conversation she'd had with Ren earlier. She didn't know why she'd been so raw, so honest. Probably because it was only, what, two, three days into their new "relationship" (or "trial run") and she was already getting overwhelmed with feelings for him?

She felt an ache in her chest. He hadn't kissed her tonight. He'd held her, and had cuddled with her on the couch, but they'd both been careful not to do anything that might set a match to the kindling of sexual tension that usually surrounded them.

Still, it didn't mean she didn't want him.

She'd told him she'd slept with other men. She liked sex, and it had been a long time since she'd had enjoyable sex with anyone. Ren was calling to her like a beacon. Even when they'd been teens, sex with him had been outstanding. Granted, part of it was being in love, but part of it was the extreme care he put into the act. He studied her like he was trying to unlock a mystery of the universe, where most men put in just enough effort to figure out how to get you to spread your legs. Ren knew all her triggers, understood every sigh and pant. He knew her language, as it were, and spoke sex with her fluently.

She hadn't had that kind of connection with anyone since.

But sex with Ren meant complications.

She growled, pulling the pillow over her head. *And the last thing I want is complications.*

She finally forced herself to get out of bed. She padded in bare feet towards the kitchen. The light in Ren's office was out, so he must've gone to bed, as well. He'd said when she turned in that he had some emails he had to go over.

He worked too hard. Not that it was her place to say anything.

It's not like you're dating him.

She walked into the kitchen, turning on the light. Trying to be as quiet as possible, she rummaged around in the cabinets until she found a drinking glass. She poured herself some filtered water from the fridge, sighing in relief.

"You okay?"

She let out a little yelp, spinning and spilling some water on the floor. "Oh!"

"It's all right."

Ren was standing there in nothing but a pair of shorts. He quickly grabbed a towel, dropping it on the floor and wiping up the offending puddle with a swipe of his foot. Then he tossed the towel in a nearby basket. "I heard you, wanted to make sure there wasn't anything you needed."

"I was thirsty." Did she sound as breathless to him as she sounded to herself?

She ate him up with her eyes. He wasn't wearing a shirt. The MMA training was doing wonders for him, she thought. He'd been fit in high school, but this was a whole new level. She could see the carved definition of his pecs. His arms were works of sculpture.

Good lord, the man even had a six-pack. She felt her mouth go dry again, and quickly gulped down more water.

"You sure you're okay?" he asked, sounding amused.

She frowned. He had to know how hot he was. *Had* to know the effect he had on women.

"I'm feeling a little robbed, actually," she said.

"Oh?"

"You said this would be a PG-13 gentleman night," she heard herself say, as she put the glass down on the counter. "And there was absolutely no making out."

Now she saw his expression go from amused to surprised to hungry in the space of a few seconds. "I didn't think you'd want to," he said.

"I'm not sure about us," she admitted. "But I do know that I'm just as attracted to you as I've ever been. Maybe more, if that's possible," she added, with a broken laugh.

"I'm still attracted to you, too. You have to know that." He stepped closer, and she could feel heat pouring off of him like a furnace.

She wanted. Wanted sex, wanted him. Badly enough that she was willing to overlook the complications that would inevitably follow.

"A little kissing wouldn't kill anybody," she said, and pressed herself against him.

Her nipples pebbled to hard points beneath the thin T-shirt material, and she dragged her chest against his abs. *Hallelujah.* Her body lit up like a pinball machine, and her breathing went shallow.

His breathing went shallow, too, and she could feel him hardening against her stomach. "You were the one that put the boundaries on us," he reminded her, disconcerting her. "No sex. I don't want you to use this as a reason why we can't be together."

She frowned. He was right, of course. Sex clouded judgement. Of course, right now her judgment was so clouded she genuinely couldn't give a shit.

"This will be separate," she said, her voice edgy with need. "Ren, I haven't had sex – good, bad, or indifferent – in over a year."

He blinked. "Oh?"

"And sex with you was always phenomenal." She squirmed a little, enjoying his groan. "I don't want to make it seem like I'm using you..."

"On second thought, please," he groaned. "Go ahead. Use me."

She let out a frustrated laugh, linking her arms around his neck as his hands smoothed down the T-shirt, grasping her hips. "But I couldn't sleep because I was thinking about you, here, just in the next room. And I was thinking of how badly I want you."

He bent down, burying his face in the crook of her neck. "Rachel," he growled.

Then, with a quick movement, he grabbed her, picking her up and putting her on a kitchen counter. His mouth found hers, devouring her.

She was grabbing at the strong yoke of his shoulders, wrapping her legs around his waist. He pressed against her pussy, pulling her to the edge of the counter. He reached into her loose sweatpants. "You're already wet," he said, when his fingers pushed her panties aside, stroking against her slit.

She couldn't find words, just mewled an agreement. She pressed hot kisses wherever she could – his chest, his neck, his jawline. His hot, hungry mouth.

"This... isn't... PG-13," he said, and his fingers moved against her clit in a way that made her gasp and her head fall back as her hips pivoted to give him better access.

"Fuck PG-13," she breathed. "Actually, just fuck *me*."

He froze, and she actually let out a cry of distress. "Rachel, are you serious?"

"*Yes*," she said, tugging his hair. "I want you, Ren."

He stared at her for a long moment. Then he kissed her again. "We'll see how far we get," he said. "I can make you happy, but still stay within your boundaries."

She frowned. Was he talking about... wait, what was he talking about?

He picked her up, taking her to his bedroom. His navy-blue sheets were rumpled, like he'd gotten out of bed. He put her down on the bed, then he grabbed the waist of the sweatpants and maneuvered the garment off of her. Then the panties. When he crouched in front of her, and she felt his hot breath against her thighs, she realized what he was doing.

"Ren," she said, then her head hit the bed when she felt his mouth, pressing delirious kisses against first one thigh, then the other. He kissed her right on her slick pussy, then parted the lips, opening her wide to his onslaught.

He licked her clit, hard, the way she liked it, and she cried out with the sheer pleasure of it, raising her hips to meet his mouth. His mouth encompassed more of her, his tongue flicking through her folds, always circling back to the hard bead of her clit. Her breathing went ragged and uneven. She reached up, grasping one breast in her palm, feeling the hard nipple poke against her. She twisted her hips in a circle, feeling the slow build of her orgasm. So much bigger than she'd gotten with her vibrator, or any of the fumbling suitors she'd settled for.

He continued to work at her, nibbling, sucking, licking with the tip of his tongue and the flat, broad surface of it, until she was chanting his name and breathing like she was running a marathon. Her hips were moving hard. Then he circled her hole with his finger before plunging it in at the same time as his mouth worked her bud.

"*Ren!*" she screamed, feeling the orgasm starting to crest. It only grew more intense as he put in a second, then a third finger, mimicking sex, filling her even as her clit was exploding with sensation. She shivered hard, feeling like she was close to blacking out, her entire body clenching.

A few minutes later, she felt like she was floating back to earth. He nuzzled her thighs, rubbing his face.

"God, I missed that," he said. "Missed you. And see? You didn't break any boundaries."

She thought about it. It was so like Ren. He was considerate. He wanted to make sure that she was happy, and that he kept his word.

She leaned up, realizing she was still wearing the T-shirt. And she saw his erection, hot and heavy and insistent, tenting his thin shorts.

She reached down, grabbing the hem of the T-shirt, and pulled it up over her head, leaving her naked in his bed.

"Let's just say this one's for sex only," she said, her voice shaking a little. "It goes outside of the boundaries of our deal. It exists in a totally different universe. What do you say?"

· ♥ · ♥ · ♥ · ♥ · ♥ ·

It's a trap.

Ren tried hard to catch his breath and organize his thinking. Rachel was lying naked in his bed, proposing a devil's bargain: sex, for this night only. And it would have nothing to do with whether or not they continued in a relationship. It would be sweaty, intense, amazing – he knew that already, just from tasting her orgasm on his tongue. His cock was throbbing like an aching tooth. His body was screaming *just have sex with her already!*

But there was a catch. There had to be a catch.

She had insisted on no sex because she didn't want to get swayed by hormones. "You've got to promise me, *if* we go through with this," he said, sounding as out of breath as if he'd just run five miles, "that you're not going to hold it against me, or say that we can't have a relationship because we had sex and somehow we weren't thinking straight."

"Ren," she said, almost a whimper of need. She writhed a little, her hips rolling. He licked his lips, and his cock twitched. "Please."

He closed his eyes. "Promise me," he said.

"I promise, I won't hold this against you," she said, propping herself up on her elbows. Her eyes blazed. "I'm a grown woman. I know I wanted to keep hormones out of this, and I think we can. At this point, I want you so badly I'm practically cross-eyed."

He barked out a laugh. "I know that feeling."

"If anything, maybe it'll help clear my mind." She looked innocent... right up until she arched her back, her breasts thrusting out towards him as she smiled coyly.

"Man, you play dirty," he said, leaning forward and taking a nipple into his mouth. He swirled his tongue around it. It was hard as a diamond, and hot. She gasped, arching higher, pressing herself deeper into his mouth. He pulled back, blowing on the wet circle and enjoying her shiver. "So, in the interest of being clear..."

"Oh, for God's sake," Rachel said, nudging against him. "Really? With all the talking?"

He stared at her until she met his gaze straight on. "I'm not losing you this time," he said, each word clear. "Even if that means I have to hold off on sex with you. I'm not a kid anymore."

She seemed to take that in. Her expression softened, and she raised one hand to stroke the side of his face. "No, you're not a kid," she said. "You're right. We should be circumspect."

He felt both elated and disappointed. Then she leaned up and kissed him, a gentle kiss that grew in intensity.

"I won't hold this against you," she said against his mouth. "I promise. You won't lose me over this."

His control snapped with those few words. He groaned, deepening the kiss, covering her body with his. She felt like she was on fire, her breasts crushed against his chest, her nipples dragging against his pecs as she squirmed beneath him. Her hands smoothed across his back, then trailed up his sides until she shimmied and wove her fingers in the back of his hair. He kept kissing her as his arms kept him propped up so he wasn't crushing her. His cock was notched between her legs, but he still had his damned boxers and shorts on.

"Shorts," he muttered against her neck. "I need to get them off."

"Yeah you do." She let go, long enough for him to disengage and quickly strip the offending articles off.

He reached for the nightstand, pulling out a drawer. He couldn't believe his hand was shaking as he pulled out a condom. Then, thinking about it, he pulled out a few more, leaving them on the surface. *Just in case.*

He started to turn back, only to see Rachel reaching for him. "Wait a second on that," she said, her expression mischievous. She circled his erection with her fingers. How the hell did her palms get so soft? It was like being stroked by a cloud. She made a little humming noise of appreciation, then leaned down, her fragrant, silky hair brushing against the length of him.

Then she wrapped her lips around him, and he closed his eyes as a huff of breath escaped him. "*Rachel.*"

She licked the head of his cock, then sucked it with gentle pressure as those soft hands stroked his shaft, cradled his balls. He couldn't help his hips pitching forward, pressing more deeply into her mouth. He didn't think it was possible for him to get harder, but his cock was like iron in her mouth. She hummed again, a happy sound that reverberated through every nerve ending.

"Not... not yet," he said, pulling out of her mouth with a wet sound. "God, you're good at that. But it's been too long, and I want to be inside you when I come."

She nodded. "All right."

He needed a few minutes of deep breathing and thinking of spreadsheets before he could calm down enough to roll on a condom. She stretched out on the bed, looking like a goddess. He covered her up again with his body, moving between her thighs. Nudging her with his hardness.

She was still slippery from her orgasm, and he slid in, but she was tight. He gritted his teeth against how good it felt. He kept pressing in, gently. She hadn't had sex in a while (*a year!* His subconscious provided with shock) so he didn't want to hurt her. But she didn't seem to be in pain. If anything, she was impatient, raising her hips to meet him, curving her legs around his. He felt his stomach stroke against hers as his cock slid all the way home, buried to the hilt in her.

They both let out simultaneous moans of pleasure. He withdrew, then moved in again, with more force, more speed. He reached between them, spreading her folds, making sure that her clit was exposed to his pubic bone, then angled to ensure that he was hitting it with every dragging thrust. She gasped, moving faster, more insistently. "Ren... *Ren*... Oh my God."

He adjusted his speed, matching hers, clenching his jaw. She felt *so good.* He could tell from the broken sound of her breathing that she was getting close.

"*Ren!*" she shouted, and he felt her pulsing around him, and she clawed at his back, her legs tense as boards, her toes curling.

He almost followed her down right there. Instead, he pulled out quickly, and flipped them over. He sat with his body against the headboard, then tugged Rachel onto his lap. Her eyes widened.

"You remembered," she breathed, then lowered herself back onto his cock. She couldn't have multiple orgasms on her back – but if they switched positions after, she could have a double, maybe even a triple.

He grinned, then sucked first one, then the other nipple, tasting her, teasing her, as she bucked her hips and rode him. She wrapped her legs around him, taking him even deeper, and he breathed hard against her neck, holding her tight to him.

"I missed you," he said against her hot velvet skin. Then he drove upward, leaving her gasping. There was a spot, her spot. He moved, sweating, his hips pistoning as he moved inside her, back and forth, up and down. She was gasping and panting, pressing against him as if she just couldn't get close enough. Their hips were moving in tandem, jarring together.

"Rachel," he pleaded, as they ground together.

She threw back her head and screamed, shivering. Her thighs tightened around him like a vise, and he felt her pussy clench like a fist around his cock.

He couldn't have stopped his orgasm with a gun to his head. In fact, it felt like he'd been shot as the pleasure cannonballed through him, leaving him momentarily speechless, lights flashing before his eyes.

She shuddered against him for a long minute. He gasped and panted against her damp skin.

"Oh my God," she breathed. "That was good."

He smiled as she clambered off, the awkwardness of post-sex somehow delightful. "That was better than good," he said, walking to the en suite bathroom and taking off the condom.

When he got back, she was grabbing her clothes. "Well," she said, her voice almost cheerful. "Goodnight."

He blinked. "Wait, what?"

"I promised I wouldn't let this affect my decision, or let it get weird," she said. "So... I'm going to go back to the guest bedroom."

Are you shitting me?

He was about to say so, when he saw the confusion and vulnerability in her eyes. She needed this ... this assertion of control. Because she still didn't trust him.

What's it going to take to change your mind?

He couldn't screw this up, though. If he moved too fast, pushed too hard, he was going to lose her. He still had a chance.

"All right," he said quietly. "But if you change your mind, I'd welcome you in here. I *want* you in here."

"Okay," she said. Then, with slow steps, she walked out and closed the door behind her.

CHAPTER 7

The next evening, Rachel called Ren from the bookstore. "Hi," he answered. "I was just thinking about you. I think I've got a date you might like."

"I'm sorry," she said quickly. "I'm not going to be able to go out tonight."

He was quiet for a second. "This isn't because of last night, is it?"

"What? No!" she said, then quickly reiterated, "No, it's not. I promise."

"Because I swear, if last night changed *anything*..."

"I said it wouldn't." She felt her cheeks heat. "We were able to pull together a girls' night tonight, and our schedules have been so all-over-the-place, getting together is a big deal. I don't want to cancel on them."

"Girls' night? Well, that sounds promising." His cheerful voice sounded a little forced. "I guess it's too much to hope for pillow fights and skimpy PJs?"

"What are we, twelve?" she asked, with a responding laugh. "It's more like movies and mojitos."

Ren chuckled, sounding a little more normal. "Okay, plans can wait. Can I still see you tomorrow?"

"Yes. Absolutely."

"And we'll add an extra day to my count," he said. "We won't include today, since you've got other plans."

"You drive a hard bargain, but okay."

"All right. I'll talk to you tomorrow." He hesitated again, his voice low and rough. And let's face it, sexy as all hell. "Is it okay to say I can't stop thinking about last night?"

She closed her eyes, her thighs clenching.

"Sorry." He sighed. "I'll... see you tomorrow."

"I've thought a lot about last night, too," she said, her voice breaking a little.

That morning, they had both had to go to work early. He'd given her a lingering kiss before sending her off with his driver. Still, neither had addressed the elephant in the room: their scorching sex the night before... and the fact that she'd retired to the guest room immediately afterward.

She was torn between feeling incredibly stupid for giving in to her hormones, and unbelievably turned on and impatient to have sex with him again.

"I'll see you tomorrow," he promised, then hung up.

She wandered down from her bedroom, wearing her comfiest fleece sweats and a giant purple sweater. She could hear her friends assembling in the store's "common area", which was basically a living room. Her friend Kyla was the first to greet her.

"It's so good to see you!" she said, throwing her arms around Rachel in a big hug. "With work and school, it feels like it's been forever. How are you doing? Other than car troubles," she added. "I got your Subaru this morning."

"Nothing too bad, I hope?"

"Just the starter, I think. Not a problem," Kyla reassured her. "The guy said he towed it from U Dub, though. That had to suck."

Ren had taken care of it for her. She felt her cheeks heat with a blush. Ren was getting far too comfortable taking care of her. *And you're getting far too comfortable letting him.*

Hailey came out with their friend Tessa and started distributing Tessa's signature hot chocolate laced with tequila. Rachel quickly grabbed one and took a long sip. *Mmmm.*

"I'm surprised Noah's not here," their other friend Mallory said, looking around. "The guy's here every time I stop by."

"He had to work tonight," Cressida said, with a smile. "He'll be by later."

"Still happy?" Mal asked curiously.

"Deliriously so." Cressida beamed.

Stacy, Rachel's best friend from high school, sat on one of the overstuffed couches and took them all in. "I can't believe we're all in relationships," she marveled. "All at the same time, I mean. That's never happened. And we're all *happy*."

"That's not quite true," Mal said. "Rache, you're still the last holdout."

"She's been dating," Hailey said, her tone a little sour.

Rachel took a deep breath. She always liked girls' night, but tonight she had a specific goal: get their advice on the Ren thing.

"I have been dating," she said slowly, then sat down next to Stacy. "I've been seeing Ren Chu again."

Silence met this remark. Then Tessa piped up, "Who's Ren Chu?"

"Her boyfriend from high school," Stacy said, with a tone of shock.

"Who absolutely broke her heart," Mallory added. "Just before he went off to college, right?"

Rachel squirmed with embarrassment and remembered pain. "Yes."

"She called him to borrow his plane when I was in the desert," Cressida said, shaking her head. "And… they just sort of connected."

"He says he wants to give us another try," Rachel said.

Another moment of shocked silence. "Wow. He's got some balls on him, huh?" Mallory said finally.

"I *know*, right?" Hailey quickly agreed. "After all this time, just to act like 'hey, sorry I was an asshole, let's give it another go?' I mean, who does he think he is?"

"Breaking up with someone doesn't make them an asshole," Kyla said, but she sounded a little unsure. "How did he break up with you?"

Before Rachel could respond, Hailey popped in. "He told her he was going to be *too busy for her*. That he wasn't going to have time for her."

"They both would've been studying," Kyla said. "Maybe..."

"He didn't prioritize her," Hailey countered. "He basically said that he had bigger things to take care of, and he had to cut her off so he could go do them."

"Did he really say that?"

Rachel bit her lip, then nodded.

The women made murmuring sounds of anger.

"What an asshole," Tessa said.

"In his defense," Rachel said, "he wasn't wrong. We were three thousand miles apart. Long distance relationships are difficult. We probably wouldn't have made it."

"But you could've tried," Kyla said. "Sounds like he didn't want to."

How could it still hurt this much after ten years? "He didn't want to," she said, in a small voice.

"So why are you dating him now?"

Rachel took a deep breath, wrapping her fingers around her mug of cocoa to comfort herself. "I don't know. At first, it was… well, it was a little for revenge," she admitted. "I wanted him to see how badass I was doing without him. Got all dressed up, the whole nine yards."

Stacy smiled. "Good for you. God, who doesn't want to get back at an ex that way?"

"But we just… clicked." Rachel felt embarrassed. "He looks even better now than he did then. And… well, before he was an asshole, he just had this way of making me feel special. He actually listened to my conversations and was emotionally supportive."

"And then hung you out to dry." Hailey crossed her arms.

"Go easy," Cressida said to Hailey, patting her shoulder. "Stop pushing."

"That's what I'm worried about now," Rachel said. "He was great… until he wasn't. Until something more important came along. I don't want to go through all that again. I don't want to let my guard down again."

The women looked at each other.

"I say don't give him the opportunity," Mallory said, shaking her head. "The guy sounds like a charmer."

"I remember what they were like together," Stacy protested. "I think that it genuinely killed him to break up with you, but he probably was doing what he thought was best. Also, I bet you anything his parents pressured him to do it. They were on his case hard to get good grades, work for the family business, all that."

"It doesn't help that they found out we'd been engaged for like a year," Rachel admitted.

"You were *what*?" Stacy yelped. "Engaged? And you didn't even tell me?"

"I didn't tell anyone, except Hailey and Cress," Rachel apologized. "We were so young. And Ren knew that his family would probably flip out about it."

"Did they?"

Rachel nodded. "Apparently. It was about a week later that we broke up. I guess they sat him down and spelled out all the difficulties that we were going to face, being so far apart, and with his studies and all."

"Did they by any chance tell rich boy that he'd be cut off from all funding if he married you?" Hailey asked.

"I don't think they had to go that far," Rachel said. "He was so intent on pleasing them, and they were so insistent... "

"So in the face of family pressure, he chickened out," Mallory said. "Definitely steer clear of this guy."

"He does still work for his family," Stacy said, sounding troubled.

Rachel sighed. She'd wanted to ask for their advice – and the consensus seemed obvious.

Leave Ren alone.

"You don't have to decide right away, do you?" Cressida said, obviously sensing her pain.

"She should cut this off sooner rather than later," Mallory said, which had Hailey nodding. "The longer she hangs out with him, the more mixed up she's going to get. And God forbid she sleeps with him."

Rachel felt her face flame. Of course, Stacy picked up on it, laughing.

"Too late, huh?"

Hailey shot her a look of disgust. "Really?"

"You, Hailey, are going to give me a lecture on having sex with somebody?" Rachel said. Before Hailey had started seeing Jake, she'd had a strict love-'em-and-leave-'em policy.

"I'd love it if you were having more sex!" Hailey scolded. "Just not with assholes who *broke your heart*!"

"Was it good, at least?" Stacy asked, with an impish grin.

Rachel grinned back. "Outstanding."

"Well, shit." Mallory smirked. "Bit too late now."

"Ultimately, it's Rachel's business," Cressida said, her voice firm. "Whether she gets hurt or not, she's a grown woman and can make her own choices." She was looking at Hailey as she said that. "It's disrespectful to assume that she can't."

Hailey looked disgruntled but nodded. "Sorry, Rachel."

Rachel shrugged. "I gave him a week," she said. "He's got seven days to convince me why I should trust him, and that I should start dating him again."

Stacy's smile was wide. "Oooh."

"I also said he couldn't spend more than fifty dollars on any date," Rachel added, feeling a little smug. "So he can't just throw a lot of money into romancing me, he's got to put thought into it."

"I approve of that," Mallory said.

"And I had a no sex clause, but… well, I wanted sex."

The women burst into laughter.

Rachel laughed with them but felt an ache in her chest. All signs pointed to no when it came to Ren.

So why did she so badly want to say *yes*?

· ♥ · ♥ · ♥ · ♥ · ♥ ·

Having nothing better to do, Ren had done work in his home office the previous night. He wished like hell he could've seen Rachel instead. He respected her desire for a girls' night, and he didn't want to pressure her. But damn it, she couldn't expect to give him one of the most memorable nights of sex in his life, and then to bounce away like it had meant nothing. He was trying to be understanding, and he *had* screwed up, but he wasn't a doormat, damn it. He didn't want what went on between them to feel cheap – and the way she'd gotten up and gone to the other room after sex had felt kind of like that.

Maybe you should talk to her about that tonight.

He closed his eyes. Tonight. He'd planned something special: something that fit under her budgetary cap, something that was (he hoped) thoughtful, something that she'd really enjoy. After that, he was torn. He didn't want sex to screw up the ultimate goal here, which was to have Rachel back in his life. But the sex... *dammmnn.* If she said "hey, want to go back to your place?" he seriously doubted he had the willpower to say "no, let's wait" just because he didn't want things to get weird again.

But maybe he was getting ahead of himself. Maybe she wouldn't want to have sex again. She said she was interested, but scared, and he wasn't sure what side of the fence she was going to land on.

"Hey, Ren? *Ren.* Earth to Ren."

He looked up to find Stephen there, looking nervous. Ren had been pissed at him since finding out he'd told Peter about keeping Ren's schedule clear for his dates with Rachel. Stephen had explained that he was trying to keep the week cleared for him, and he couldn't come up with another plausible reason Peter would understand. Ren forgave him, but he was still irritated.

"What is it?"

Stephen winced. "Um, your parents wanted to know if you have a few minutes to check in, in your father's office."

Ren frowned. "Do you know why?"

"No idea."

Ren glanced at his computer. He wasn't working on anything that couldn't wait for a bit, he decided. He strolled out of his office, then took the elevator all the way to the top floor. His father's floor, since it only housed his father's office, the offices of his father's three assistants, and a few miscellaneous meeting rooms.

"Hello, Mr. Ren," Lorraine, his father's primary assistant, said with a warm smile as he stepped out of the elevator. "Your family's waiting in the sapphire room."

"Thanks." His *family*?

He headed over to one of the smaller conference rooms, one with a great view of the ocean. His parents were there, as were his younger brother Jian, and his younger sister, Meili.

"What's going on?" he asked, feeling a little blindsided. "Was there something scheduled that I forgot about? We're still meeting for brunch this weekend, aren't we?"

"Actually, we're not," his father said. "I'm taking your mother to New York for the weekend. So we thought we'd catch up now, quickly. We know you're all very busy."

"I did have to shift a meeting," Jian said, sounding a little irritated. His mother glared at Jian, who quickly fell silent.

"I need to get back to my sales calls," Meili said. At twenty-three, she was the baby of the family, and she'd been working in sales at the highly successful cell phone component division. She was making good numbers, but still had a way to go before becoming a top earner. Or at least, that's what his parents seemed to zero in on.

"Speaking of flying to New York," his father said, with deceptive calm, "it came to my attention that you used the plane about a month ago, Ren. Or at least, you let someone use it."

They all focused on him. He felt uncomfortably like a child being called up to the principal's office at school. Of course, he'd often felt like that with his parents.

Not that he'd ever been to the principal's, other than to receive some kind of commendation. His parents would have killed him.

"Anything you'd like to tell me?" his father prompted.

Ren tilted his head, studying his father. "I thought that we all had use of the planes, as long as they were available."

"Of course we do. But you didn't mention anything about it."

Ren tightened his jaw. Not that it was any of their business – but this was the Chu family. *Everything* was their business, and after nearly thirty years, he knew better. "I loaned it to a friend. Her sister was having a medical emergency, and needed to get home immediately."

"Oh, my," his mother said, genuine concern on her face. "Is she all right?"

"She seems to be fine now. They send their appreciation." Actually, Rachel would probably still offer money if he let her.

"*Her* sister." His father picked up on the pronoun. "Who? Which friend?"

He knew that if he tried something like saying "does it really matter?" would only be waving a bone in front of a dog. "Rachel. Frost."

Silence reigned. He could see the exact moment the memory of exactly who Rachel Frost was hit his parents. Since Jian already knew, he was trying as best he could to look impassive. Meili still looked puzzled.

"Who's Rachel Frost?"

"His girlfriend. *Ex-girlfriend*. From high school," their mother explained. "So. You were helping her and her sister with a medical emergency?"

He nodded.

His father stared at him. "She's the one you're dating now, then? The one you've been seeing?"

Jian shot him a look that said: *you are so boned, dude.*

"I don't see how it's relevant, but yes. I've gone out on a few dates with Rachel. Like I said, it's new, and we're taking it slow." Way slower than he wanted to, that was for sure.

His mother sighed. "Do you really think that's wise?"

"Why wouldn't it be?"

"People change a lot in a decade," she said gently. "She may not be the girl you remember. And even if she was, you've changed. Do you really think you're... compatible?"

"Only one way to find out," Ren said easily, feeling trapped. Jian and Meili were looking on like spectators at the Indy 500, witnessing a particularly horrific car pile-up. "Please tell me you didn't pull a meeting together just to talk to me about my social life."

His father locked gazes with his, scowling. Ren didn't back down. Finally, his father let out a long exhalation.

"No. We talked with some of the CEOs and COOs, and we're going to be making some changes. The Electronics Division is in a downward spiral and needs to be fixed as soon as possible."

Ren grimaced. "Working on it."

"Well, you'll have help." His father turned to Jian. "From now on, you're going to be helping Ren."

"I already help Ren. Over in internal security."

"You're moving to operations," his father clarified.

Jian's eyes widened. "I don't generally work in operations," he said carefully. "I mean, computer security and auditing are a subset of operations, I suppose, but..."

"You're going to work directly with your brother. He isn't getting the information he needs, and he'll need a right-hand man that is actively getting the information disseminated."

"What, am I his assistant?" Jian spluttered.

His father's cool gaze made him quiet down.

"Meili," their mother said, "the sales for the Electronics Division have been terrible. We think you'll best be able to help there."

Ren saw the aghast look on his sister's face before she quickly masked it. "The sales are terrible because the sales software is still broken," she said, obviously trying to hide her panic. "And because the inventory software doesn't work well either, we aren't shipping on time or in sufficient quantities to our current customers."

"So, you know the issues at hand," her mother said. "You'll be able to work around them and show the sales team how they should be handling the challenges."

Ren could practically see his sister's crumbling disappointment. She wasn't going to be hitting those target numbers this year, either.

"Ren," his father finally said, "you're going to get the factory at Zhuhai straightened out, you're going to get the software issues dealt with, and we're all going to have the Electronics Division running like it should be before the end of the year. End of discussion."

Ren nodded curtly. He saw why this was happening on his father's floor, and not at some chichi brunch. This was a family meeting, yes, but it was *business*. All three kids were now going into battle, having been given their marching orders.

"We'll let you get back to your day," their mother said, smiling like a genial hostess. "I'm sure you've got maneuvering you need to do. Meili, your supervisor's been notified, and you'll move over next week, all right? And Jian, Peter will have an office waiting for you."

Knowing he'd been dismissed, Ren got up and went to the elevator, flanked by his siblings. When they got into the elevator, Jian exploded.

"What the *hell* was that?"

"It was like a contract hit," Meili said, covering her face with her hand. "*Electronics Division*? I am going to make *no* money this year. This sucks!"

"They want me to be your sidekick?" Jian was practically shaking. "Could somebody tell me what that's supposed to accomplish?"

Ren let them vent, then held up a hand when they got to his floor. "Listen, it'll be okay," he said, holding the door. "This is the squeaky wheel. We're the maintenance crew, that's all."

"Maintenance, my ass," Jian said.

Ren sent him a tired smile. "We'll get through it. We always do, don't we?"

They grumbled at him. He let the door go.

He trudged back to his office. The thing was, his parents didn't give much thought to what their kids needed or wanted. It was the good of the company, always. To them, there weren't really boundaries, or privacy, or life separate from Chu Enterprises. It was one big, seamless entity.

God, he wanted to see Rachel. He wanted something, someone, of his own.

He looked at the work on his computer. More emails, he thought. More headaches. More fires to put out. And no doubt more people would be "popping by" his office, or Peter would try and set up yet another pointless meeting.

"Stephen," he said, grabbing his coat and slipping his laptop into his bag, "I'm going to work from home this afternoon."

"You are?" Stephen sounded vaguely scandalized. "Um... okay."

Damned straight okay, Ren thought rebelliously. Then he walked out the door... and shut off his phone.

· ♥ · ♥ · ♥ · ♥ · ♥ ·

"So, what kind of wild shenanigans do you have planned for this evening?" Rachel asked, as she climbed into Ren's car. "Night at the races? Breaking and entering? A vicious game of Scrabble?"

"Monopoly's always been more my speed," Ren said. "But no, I thought we'd go traditional with a twist tonight. It might be a touch over your budget, but I think we can manage."

"Ren..." she said warningly, but she caught the dimple as he smiled, not turning from his view of the road.

"Just a touch, seriously. But it'll be worth it."

He looked a little tired, she noticed. She wondered if she should say anything.

"How was girls' night?"

"It was fun," she said. "Women need other women to hang out with. I'm lucky I'm still in touch with my friends from high school. And we made some new friends, too. Hanging out with them grounds me." She shook her head. "Guys don't have that."

"I think guys expect that from the women they're with," Ren mused.

"Or they have that from their families," she said.

She saw the smile slip from Ren's face. Aha. Family trouble. Recent, she wondered? Or just in general?

"Anyway, it was fun."

"Did you talk about me?" Now he looked at her quickly, wiggling his eyebrows.

If you only knew...

"What happens at girls' night," she said sanctimoniously, "stays at girls' night."

He chuckled softly.

After a little bit, they arrived at their destination: one of those movie theaters that was more like a restaurant. You could watch the movie from a couch, and they served pizza.

"Oh my God," Rachel breathed. "I've always meant to go to one of these, but I never have. How'd you know?"

"You told me you wanted to go to one of these places back in high school. I'm surprised you still haven't been, actually. I was afraid you were totally a regular here."

She nudged him, and he put his arm around her shoulders as they walked up to the building. He got their tickets. She let out a small squeal when she saw what they were playing.

"*The Mummy*, with Brendan Fraser?" She gave him a quick squeeze. "I can't believe it! I *love* that movie!"

"I know," Ren said, sounding amused. "That's why I took you here."

She blinked. He really did remember, she thought. That had always been her downfall. He did these thoughtful little gestures, things that other boys – and men – just didn't seem to notice or care about. He put her first.

I want to trust you...

The restaurant/theater, such as it was, had couches strewn everywhere, with small round tables in front of them. It wasn't very crowded. There were some college-aged kids who had taken over a corner by the front and were splitting a large pizza with everything. A few other couples had taken couches around the center. Ren nudged her towards the back, and they placed their order.

"Movie'll start in a few minutes," the waitress said.

Rachel sat with her back against the couch. Ren casually put his arm around her shoulders. "How was your day?" he asked.

She told him about her car and its starter problem, how Hailey had driven her to work (because nobody drives Hailey's car but Hailey, for a variety of reasons), and how one of their acts, an up-and-coming comedian, was driving her nuts with his demands. "And how about you?" she asked. "How was your day?"

She saw it again, the tension in his expression. "Frustrating," he said. And left it there.

She frowned. "You know, if you want to have a relationship, you're going to have to actually open up a bit," she pointed out. "If I'm in, I'm in. That means bad stuff, not just you spoon-feeding me good news and then bottling up any negative emotions. That's a recipe for disaster."

"I know," he said.

"Then spill." She looked at him expectantly.

"My parents..." He let out an irritated sigh. "They expect a lot from me. I'm okay with that. They've stuck me in the worst division in the corporation, one that's having a lot of problems, and they're expecting me to pull off miracles to get everything resolved."

"That's why you go in at ten o'clock at night," she said. "That's why you went back to your home office the other night, after I went to bed."

"Well, part of that was to get my mind off the fact that you were just feet away from me, and probably naked," he admitted, and she giggled. "But yeah. There's been a ton of work. One of our factories is in China, so it opens after we close. But I could work a twenty-hour day if I didn't need sleep... and I think, sometimes, that my parents would have me do that if they thought I could without losing my sanity."

Rachel bit her lip. That sounded awful.

"You probably know what that's like," he said. "You're kind of working two jobs, with school and your job at the casino. You know it can be stressful."

"Yeah, but there's a light at the end of my tunnel," she pointed out. "I graduate in June. How long can you keep this up?"

"I'm hoping once the problems get resolved, I'll be able to work more normal hours."

She wondered if he realized he sounded doubtful.

Their burgers arrived, and they looked *good*. Rachel felt her stomach growl.

"Are you always hungry? Don't you eat?"

Rachel bit into her burger. It was as delicious as it appeared. "Shut up," she said around a mouthful. He laughed, then tucked into his own burger as the movie started.

She had a blast. She'd always loved this movie, in all its cheesy goodness. Brendan Fraser was a hottie, and Rachel Weisz was both adorable and badass. "I… am… a *librarian!*" Rachel murmured along with Evie on the screen.

Ren hugged her to him. She couldn't help herself. She leaned over, kissing him. "Thank you," she breathed.

He kissed her back, gently.

She kissed him again.

He stroked her back.

The kiss grew a little more… insistent.

She closed her eyes, pressed a little harder against him.

Suddenly, they heard a low whistle. She jerked back, only to see the college-aged crew looking back at them. A few were giving thumbs up.

She felt like her cheeks were on fire. She looked up at Ren, who was grinning at her. *Oops*, he mouthed.

She buried her head against his cheek for a minute. The kiss had been nice – an appetizer.

Unfortunately, it had also called up memories of the last time she'd been at his house. Those kisses had been more than nice. They had been downright *incendiary.*

Not to mention the skin-on-skin connection.

Oh, and his *tongue.*

She tried to stay focused on the movie. Her body was already running down memory lane by this point, reminding her of the night before – and of all the other times they'd been together. That night after Homecoming, when he'd gone down on her in the car for the first time. Or when he'd let her tie him up and blindfold him when his parents had been out of town, and his brother and sister had been gone. Memory after memory washed over her, making her pussy throb. She squirmed.

"You okay?" Ren breathed in her ear. The sensation of his lips so close to the sensitive skin made her quiver, and all she could do was nod.

She barely registered that the movie had stopped, but it was over. "You have a good time?" Ren asked.

She ignored the grins on the faces of the college kids, and instead turned to him. "I had a great time," she said. *Now let's go back to your place.*

He must've been feeling it, too, because he leaned down to kiss her, hard. "I'll be honest," he said. "I wasn't really paying attention. I'm just glad I was with you. Being with you makes me feel better."

Gah! Right in the feels, again!

She closed her eyes. Here she was, being a total horn-dog, and he was being sentimental. She kissed him back. Then they walked to the car.

"I suppose I ought to take you home," he said, but the words sounded open ended.

"I totally feel like seeing *The Mummy Returns* now," she said. "It's not as good as the first one, but it's still sweet. And I love the romance between Rick and Evie."

Ren's eyes flashed for a second. "Want to see it at my place?"

Her various body parts immediately chimed in their assent. *Damn, that sounds like a* fine *idea!*

She cleared her throat. "It's going to be late if I go over to the city with you now," she said.

"True." He sounded disappointed.

"So… maybe I should grab a few things from home," she ventured. Then waited for him to put it together.

He stood straighter. Then he held her, turning her to look at him. "If you stay with me tonight, we're going to have sex."

She let out a surprised peal of laughter. "I know. I don't really want to watch the sequel that badly," she admitted.

"If we have sex again, I don't want to pretend like it didn't happen." He looked pained. "I get that you're scared, and that you want to take it slow. I even get if you want to keep the sex separate from... whatever it is that we may or may not be starting. But pretending it didn't happen is shitty, okay? You wouldn't put up with it if I did it to you, and I wouldn't expect you to."

She felt a pang. "You're right. I'm sorry, Ren."

He nodded. "Apology accepted."

She waited. "So where does that leave us?"

He kissed her, hard, body pressing her against his car. When she came up for air, they were both breathing hard.

"Now," he said, "we go to your house, *really fast,* and then back to mine."

Rachel felt every nerve ending tingling. That was probably stupid, but right now, it felt really, really good.

CHAPTER 8

Ren felt both nervous and excited as he brought Rachel back to his place again. There had been a little awkwardness as she'd packed up a small bag to take to his place. Cressida had been there, and he'd met her boyfriend, Noah, who seemed friendly enough. He thought he'd heard Cressida whisper to Rachel "are you sure about this?" and Rachel hadn't quite nodded. She'd shrugged, then given her sister a hug.

He wanted her to be sure about it. About *them*. He knew it was too early.

That said, he hoped they were making progress.

As soon as he got her through the door, he wanted to body press her against a wall and take her mouth, kissing her hard. But he didn't. He took her coat, hanging it up on a hook, and hung up his own.

"It's early yet," he said, glancing at a clock. It was only ten. "Do you want to see if I can find *The Mummy Returns*? I'll bet I could get it on demand or streaming somewhere..."

"You don't have to entertain me," she said, and she seemed a little nervous, too. She stroked his cheek, then rubbed her hand down the front of his chest. "Besides, we both know I'm not here to watch a movie."

His heart beat double time. "I didn't want to just jump on you as soon as we walked inside," he said.

"I wouldn't have minded." Her smile was both sexy and sweet.

With that, the gloves were off. He reached for her, and she reached right back. He wrapped his arms around her, pulling her tight against him as his mouth moved over hers, tasting her, testing her. She sighed against him, pressing her breasts against his chest, her pelvis rolling lightly against his quickly hardening erection.

He probably should've been going more slowly, he thought absently. Then the overwhelming sensation of Rachel in his arms hit him, and he became incapable of coherent thought entirely. His hands roamed over her back, her hips, that glorious ass of hers. She let out a low groan as he squeezed, pulling her against him. She bit his lower lip, a sharp nip, and he retaliated by sucking her lip, then teasing the sensitive inner flesh with his tongue. Their tongues twined from there. She was gripping his shoulders tightly.

"Bedroom," she gasped, pulling away from him. "*Now.*"

He smirked against her, then picked her up. She let out a small squeak, then wrapped her legs around his waist. He carried her over to his bedroom. He could feel the heat from her, through their layers of clothes. He wanted nothing but skin between them.

He tossed her onto the bed playfully, and she bounced with a yelp and a responding laugh. "You look like you want to eat me up," she said, her eyes glowing.

He growled like a wolf, and she squealed. Then he reached for her skirt. "Maybe I *do* want to eat you up." With a deft motion, he unzipped the side zipper, tugging the garment free until she was just in a set of lavender panties. He tugged them off, leaving just her, neatly trimmed and already damp.

He didn't wait to take any of the rest of her clothes off. He simply dove between her thighs, startling her. He loved the scent of her: arousal and femininity, and a perfume that was pure Rachel. He took a deep breath, then nuzzled her, licking at her thighs in slow circles that had her panting. He stroked her folds with his fingers.

The phone rang.

"What the hell?" He'd turned his phone off. He frowned, looking around. Where the hell was that sound coming from?

"You still have a land line?" she said, sounding out of breath.

"Just for emergencies," he said.

"Then... you should answer it?" She sounded confused.

"I mean, it's for if I have an emergency and I can't use my cell phone." He turned back to her. "Just ignore it. I turned my cell off. I want to focus on you tonight."

"If you're sure..."

To show her how sure he was, he leaned down, licking her clit, circling it with his tongue. She gasped, arching. He waited until the small nub was hard and erect, then he sucked it, varying the pressure, enjoying how she was clutching the covers beneath her.

The phone stopped.

"Ren," she breathed, her hips rolling against his mouth, picking up tempo. He sucked harder, his finger plunging inside her. He could feel the flesh clenching around him, and thought about how good it would feel when it was his cock there inside her...

The phone rang again.

You have got to be kidding me.

"Ren...?"

He worked her over until she was panting hard, her breathing uneven. Then with a quick nip and several long sucks, he felt her orgasm catch. She cried out, her hands woven in his hair, pressing him hard against her wet heat. He was pumping slightly against the bed in response. He waited until she came down, then sat up, wiping his mouth.

The phone rang *again*.

"What. The actual. Fuck." He glared at the bedroom door. "I'm sorry. I have to see what this is."

"Yeah. Okay," Rachel said, catching her breath.

He stalked to the office and the landline, answering the phone on the fourth ring. "Hello?" he barked out.

"Are you dead?" Jian asked. "Because your fucking phone's been off all afternoon, and nobody's been able to get a hold of you."

"I was plowing through emails. I can't get stuff done with all the interruptions. And then I had a date tonight."

"The lead engineer at the Zhuhai factory quit today," Jian informed him. "Peter's having apoplexy. Is that still a thing? He looks like he's going to have an aneurysm. He also thinks that it's your problem, which makes it *my* problem. And Mom and Dad are none too happy that you're AWOL when the shit comes down, especially after our little talk this morning."

Fuck. Of all the times for a work crisis to come up...

But aren't work crises always *coming up?*

He grimaced. "Well, what am I supposed to do about it now? Why are you calling my house continually?"

"They set up a conference call with the Zhuhai brass. It's still going on," Jian said. "You've got time to get over here. Mom and Dad are already here."

"Now?" He thought of Rachel in the other room, her warm taste still on his tongue.

"You're already in the shit," Jian said. "You're only going to make it worse if you don't come."

Ren felt anger and resentment start to well up in him, then shift over to brittle acceptance. "I'll be there as soon as I can," he said sharply, then hung up.

How the hell am I going to explain this to Rachel?

He walked back to the bedroom. Rachel had stripped off the rest of her clothes, he noticed immediately, and was stretched out invitingly on his bedspread.

"Everything okay?" she asked.

He swallowed hard as his cock tightened like a bowstring. He would give up anything to stay in bed, here, with this woman.

But he had responsibilities. And he couldn't walk away.

"I have to go into the office," he heard himself say.

Her mouth dropped open. "Seriously? *Now?*"

"There's a sort of work emergency at Zhuhai," he said. "That's our factory near Macau, the one I was telling you about. Anyway, they're having a conference call, and I need to be on it."

She turned pink, and he realized – she was embarrassed. She quickly moved to grab her clothes.

"No! No," he said. Begged, really. "Please stay. I doubt it'll be longer than an hour. And then I'll pick up where I left off, all right?"

She glared at him.

"I know, this sucks. It's awkward, and the timing's terrible. Make yourself at home: watch whatever you want, eat whatever you want. I promise, I'll come back as soon as I can."

She looked at him. "Is it always going to be like this, Ren?"

He blinked at her. "I seriously doubt it."

"But you're not sure?"

He frowned. He'd had girlfriends – okay, more fuck buddies – that had commented on his work hours before.

Was this going to be the state of his relationships... always taking a backseat to his work?

"I'll be back soon," he said instead, kissing her. The feel of her was almost enough to make his will buckle, to the point where he thought about calling Jian back and telling him fuck the conference call. He was staying with Rachel.

He pulled away, sighing. Then he got his coat and bag and headed to the office.

· ♥ · ♥ · ♥ · ♥ · ♥ ·

I can't believe he left.

Rachel was wearing one of Ren's T-shirts and sweatpants, curled up on his bed, watching TV. He had a nice flat screen mounted against the wall, and it had taken her a little bit to figure out the controls, but eventually she'd been able to crack into the vast number of cable channels he had. She was flipping back and forth between a cooking competition and *John Wick*. Watching Keanu kick ass and look awesome fit her mood completely.

She wanted to kick some ass. Specifically, Ren's.

Part of her was still embarrassed that, despite her being there *naked* and laid out like a buffet for him, he'd still grabbed his stuff and headed in to work. It was too close to the old pain. She felt like she wasn't good enough, wasn't a high enough priority to stay with.

At least he'd gotten her off. He'd left her on the edge without an orgasm, she'd have called an Uber and headed back to Snoqualmie by now. Possibly trashing his room first before she left.

No, you wouldn't.

Well, she wouldn't have trashed his room, she thought as Keanu spoke in Russian on the TV. But she would've considered it.

It was now one in the morning. She had work. She needed to get some sleep.

She shut off the TV and was about to turn off the light when she heard the key jostling in the lock. She held the covers up tight against her chest. "Ren?"

"Yeah, it's me." She heard him drop keys in a bowl by the door, then rummage around in the office. "Sorry I'm so late."

She pulled her lips together in a tight line. Oh, he hadn't even *begun* to be sorry.

Then she got a good look at him.

He looked exhausted. "We had to hash out a replacement for our lead engineer, and there were... well, tempers got involved," he said. "And my parents wanted to chew me out for not being available when there was a work emergency, so there's that."

"What, are you supposed to be on call twenty-four-seven?" Rachel asked.

"In a nutshell: yes." Ren shook his head.

"That's bullshit. You're not a brain surgeon."

Ren blinked, then laughed softly. "Thank you."

"I'm not saying what you do isn't hard. I'm sure it is," Rachel said. "It's just not an on-call position. The world wasn't going to end if you guys were without a – what was it? Lead engineer? – for a day, right?"

"That's been my assertion," Ren said.

"So you're not drawing boundaries," Rachel said staunchly, her irritation with him shifting to his job a little. Just a little. "You need to say that what they're doing isn't healthy."

He smiled at her. "It's not that easy," he said.

"Actually, it can be that easy."

"Remember how Hailey used to get all up in your business, and I told you to tell her to knock it off? And you told me it was complicated because it was family?" Ren asked.

Rachel bit her lip. Okay, he had a point there.

"If it weren't my family, maybe it'd be different. But they are my family," he said slowly. "I love them. I want to live up to their expectations of me. It's hard, and yeah, there's definitely dysfunction. But it's what I've got."

Rachel hugged her knees to her chest. "I almost left," she blurted out. "I couldn't believe you just turned me away."

"I didn't want to." He was at her side in a blink, it seemed. "God, you have no idea how badly I wanted to stay. I just... *couldn't*."

She sighed. And that was the problem, wasn't it?

"Let me make it up to you."

"You're tired, and we both have work in the morning," she said.

He leaned forward, brushing a kiss across her lips. "Let me at least try?"

She'd stayed in his bed, hadn't she? Some part of her wanted this. She'd been *waiting* for this. "I suppose it's the least I can do," she said wryly.

He grinned at her, and some of the exhaustion melted away.

She let him tug off the T-shirt she was wearing, and she shimmied out of the sweats. Then she watched as he took off his shirt and slipped out of his shoes, slacks, boxers and socks. In no time at all, he was standing there, naked and sculpted. She didn't know where to look first: at the slopes of his pecs or the ripple of his abs, the thickness of his thighs or the proud jut of his erection.

He looked delicious. She just wanted to reach out and take a bite.

He reached for her first, stroking her face with both hands, then sliding down, cupping her breasts. She sighed with pleasure as he coaxed her nipples to life, hardening the rosy peaks beneath his palms. He leaned down, kissing her throat, nipping at the sensitive skin. Then he turned her around.

"Your back," he said. "Still an erogenous zone?"

She shivered. "You tell me," she breathed.

So few of her lovers had figured that out. Her back, her spine, was one of the most sensitive parts on her... and received the least attention. He pressed hot kisses against each vertebra, it seemed, blowing heat and dampness against her flesh and making her shiver against him. She could feel his erection pressing against her ass as he molded himself to her, stroking her sides, then down to her hips. He reached in front of her, slicking his finger down her slit, then back up, brushing against her clit, then swirling around it. She gasped. So many sensations. She was in sensory overload.

He pressed her forward gently, and she rested her head against the pillow as he tugged her hips, her ass high in the air. She heard the tearing of a foil packet and knew he was rolling on a condom. Then she felt him enter her from behind, slowly and firmly, and she wanted to scream with the slow, drowning pleasure of it.

"God, Rachel," Ren rasped as he withdrew, making her whimper at the loss. Then he pushed forward again, his cock filling her. She found herself pushing back against him, wanting to take him as deep as she could. He reached around, rubbing her clit as his hips slowly picked up the pace.

"Ren," she breathed, her hips wiggling, her thighs clenched together. His legs were outside of hers, holding her steady, keeping her channel tight. Soon, he was starting to lose some of his finesse, the pressure increasing as his body pounded into hers, his fingers working frantically against her.

She felt the orgasm starting to build. She was breathing like a marathon runner, slamming back against him, meeting him thrust for thrust, wriggling uncontrollably. When it finally hit, it detonated like a bomb.

"*Ren!*" she cried out, convulsing around him.

He released her clit, which could take no more sensation at that point. He grabbed her hips and kept pulling her to him, ramming her relentlessly, pulling almost all the way out and then driving home. She tightened herself around him and was rewarded with his groan and a resulting clumsiness. He was too far gone to notice or care.

They were like animals, mating mindlessly, raging against each other. When he pounded into her with one final thrust, she felt another orgasm pop through her, surprising her. She yelled when he did, and she felt him shudder inside her, his cock thrashing even as her walls clenched around him madly.

They both collapsed onto the bed. She hadn't felt like that since... well. She hadn't felt like that *ever*. Not even with Ren, before.

He rolled off to the side, taking her with him. He kissed her neck, making her shiver. "Let me go take care of this," he breathed, then withdrew. She let out a small disappointed sigh. She liked the feel of him inside her.

He went to the bathroom and took care of the condom, then came back to bed. "Stay here tonight," he said.

"I'm certainly not going home," she said, with a yawn, feeling deliciously worn out. "You've definitely made it up to me. I'm glad I waited."

"I mean stay *here*," he emphasized slowly. "In my bedroom. Spend the night in here with me."

She froze. She didn't want to make him feel cheap, or used. But she was getting too close to him. She knew the pitfalls of Ren: that he was great, until he had other priorities. And if tonight had been any indication, there would always be the family business as a huge "other priority."

Staying with him would be even stupider than having sex with him, she realized.

He put his arms around her. "Please," he murmured.

She took a deep breath.

"All right," she said, and wondered just how badly this was going to hurt before it was all through.

Ren knew he'd fucked up when his parents called him to their house the next morning. He'd already gotten an earful the previous night, but that had been at the office, and it was the middle of the night. Now, they were calling for a command performance. They wanted him to show up for lunch at their house. It was in the same community as Bill Gates, a rich, high-toned area. It took a while in Seattle traffic to get there, time he could've been working on the Zhuhai problems, but he knew better than to ignore it.

When he arrived, his parents' housekeeper took his coat and directed him to the dining room. His parents were there. He wondered if they decided to stay home from the office because they were up so late the night before, or because they didn't want anyone else to be privy to their conversation.

If they were going to dress down their recalcitrant son, they wouldn't want people from outside the family to hear, he guessed.

His parents were already sitting at one end of the long table, his father at the end, his mother at his father's right hand. They looked at him expectantly.

"Ren." His mother's voice was… ugh. The "I'm not angry, I'm disappointed" tone was woven through it like thread. She gestured to a seat. "Sit down."

He glanced at the plate in front of him. It looked like some kind of salad. "Thanks." He sat.

His father was simply glaring at him. He stabbed at some lettuce. "You turned your phone off." The words were laced with disbelief. "All this... this chaos going on, and you *turned your phone off.*"

"I was still available via email yesterday afternoon," Ren said.

"You had your phone turned off during the day, too?" his father barked.

Ren sighed. Obviously, he wasn't winning this one.

"Your doorman says that you brought a young woman home last night," his father said.

Ren blinked. First Stephen, now his *doorman*? "Dad, that's none of your business."

His parents goggled. His mother's eyes widened. "How could it *not* be our business?" she asked. "You ignored our phone calls all evening. What if it had been a medical emergency? Would you have said you were with a woman, and that made missing one of us dying *all right*?"

He winced as that guilt trip stabbed him. "It wasn't a medical emergency, though, was it?" he tried.

"Next time it might be," she shot back. "But what we're saying is, you thought a woman was more important than your family. You shut us out, presumably so you could..."

"Have sex," his father said bluntly.

"This is *really* not your business," Ren snapped.

"No one is saying you're not going to sleep with women," his father said, and Ren felt like dying of embarrassment for a second. "But there are more important things."

"I'm not just *sleeping* with Rachel," Ren said sharply. "I want to be in a relationship with her!"

That bomb dropped with just about the response he would've expected. His parents traded looks of concern, then turned back to him.

"How long has this been going on?" his mother asked quietly. "I thought you said you had just gone out on a few dates."

It was like high school all over again. Ren sighed. "Just a week," he said.

His father scoffed. "You don't know what you want, then," he pronounced easily. "And it's not a relationship. You've barely seen the woman."

"We were together for three years in high school."

"You were children," his mother pointed out.

"We're not anymore."

His mother's lips pursed tightly. "It's a bit difficult to tell from your actions," she rebuked. "You ignore meetings, prompting the chief operating officer to call us in. Then you tell your assistant to clear your week, simply for her. You shut your phone off, prompting your brother to hunt you down, because you ignore a work crisis." Her nostrils flared slightly. "We would not find this acceptable in anyone working for our company. Do you think you're going to get preferential treatment because you're our son? We didn't raise you to be so spoiled!"

Ren winced. He could get into the minutiae, but he knew it was a losing battle. "I'm not going to stop seeing her," he said instead. "I'm sorry if you're not happy about that."

"I wouldn't give a damn, if your work wasn't suffering for it," his father said.

"Is it really suffering, though?" Ren asked, thinking of Rachel's words the previous night. There needed to be some healthier boundaries. "Did we *really* need to have an emergency meeting last night?"

Now his parents looked at him aghast. "What is *wrong* with you?" his father asked, sounding shocked.

"Are you suggesting we simply ignore a problem and hope it gets fixed?" his mother added.

"No. I'm saying, a full night's sleep on all our parts would have probably helped."

His father shook his head. "You should know better. If there's a problem, it gets addressed. Period. That's how we work."

Ren sighed. "Maybe we can work smarter, not harder."

"Maybe we work smart *and* hard," his mother countered, "and we actually get a lead engineer in Zhuhai before March."

Another losing battle. "The problem in Zhuhai will be taken care of by the end of the year," he said, relenting. "And I'm sorry I turned off my phone, but I still think that you both are blowing my relationship with Rachel out of proportion."

"So it's not that serious?" his father asked eagerly.

"No, it is serious," Ren said. "But it's not a threat."

His father harrumphed, and his mother looked worried.

"Aren't you two headed to New York this weekend?" Ren asked. "You understand. A little time away won't kill the company."

"We are always available," his mother said. "And we can fly back at a moment's notice."

"Besides, we'll be talking with some investors while we're out there," his father said.

"Of course you are," Ren murmured, shaking his head. *Because it was always about business.*

"We're probably going to need you to go to Zhuhai and deal with the factory problems yourself, firsthand, sometime soon," his father said.

Ren nodded. He'd been expecting this. There were too many things that conference calls weren't covering. A business trip was going to have to happen, probably in the next few weeks.

Rachel had never been to Asia, he wagered. Zhuhai wasn't all that sexy, but he could take her to see Macau, and take her around. She might enjoy it. He wondered absently if she could get some time off.

"So you're going to need to stay focused," his father said, interrupting his reverie. "That is my biggest problem with this... *Rachel.* You have lost your focus."

"I'm still focused, Dad."

His father shook his head, looking at his mother, who nodded. "Prove that to us," he said, sharply. "Now. Let's eat lunch."

CHAPTER 9

"So... family meeting, huh?" Rachel said, as Hailey drove her home from work. "Sounds serious."

"It's not that big a deal," Hailey said. "It's just... I think we've all got some stuff we need to talk about."

Rachel bit her lip, trying not to worry. She'd already run the gauntlet with girls' night, and she knew already that Hailey was against Ren, and Cressida was worried. And then she'd gone and packed a bag and spent the night at the guys' house. Not that she had to answer to her sisters, obviously, she told herself. But she knew that they had valid concerns.

I could tell them it's just sex.

She sighed. But she knew that'd be a lie. The sex was amazing, and if it were anyone else, then yes, she could make the argument. But it was *Ren*. Being with him meant something.

Hailey pulled up to the house, and they both walked inside. Cressida had hot cocoas ready for them, non-alcoholic this time. "Hey, Rachel," she said, hugging her. "I'm assuming you're going out tonight?"

"Um, yes," Rachel answered. "I told him I'd go out with him every night this week, until I decided one way or another if we're going to, you know, continue. As a couple."

"How's that going?" Cressida sounded genuinely curious.

Some of Rachel's resolve started to crumble. "I don't know," she answered. "Parts of it are *really* good..."

"The sex." Hailey looked smug.

Rachel chuffed out a breath. "Then parts of it are confusing."

"That'd be the emotions," Cressida said. "Well, you'll figure it out."

Rachel wanted to say more, but she suddenly got a good look at Cressida's face, and saw that her sister was dancing with nerves – and it had nothing to do with Ren.

"What's going on?" Rachel asked.

Cressida looked at Hailey. "You want to start?"

Start? Start what?

Hailey actually looked a little unnerved, as well – which, for her amazingly confident sister, was a distinct novelty. "I have some news."

Rachel felt her stomach drop. "Are you pregnant?"

Hailey's eyes went round as dinner plates. "What? *No!* God!" She held a hand to her flat stomach. "We aren't even thinking of that for a few years yet!"

Now it was Rachel's turn to goggle. "You've talked about *kids*?" Just getting Hailey to commit had been a big step.

"Well, yeah," Hailey said, and her cheeks reddened. "We've talked about a future together. And I guess we're ready to take the next step."

Rachel felt unaccountably dense. "The next step being..."

"We're moving in together." Hailey said the words quickly, in a mush, like *we'removingintogether.*

"You're moving in together?" Rachel repeated, wanting to be sure she was clear.

"Yes. I mean, I'm over there practically every night anyway," Hailey said defensively. "He's asked me for months, and I just felt strange leaving you guys. But now that Cressida's bought the place, it's not like you need my rent. And..."

"And you want to be with your guy," Cressida said, with a wide, delighted smile.

"Yeah. I want to be with him, all the time," Hailey said. "We've talked about getting married. It makes me a little woozy, but I think I like it."

Rachel felt a pang of happiness. "Oh, that's wonderful, Hailey. Congratulations." She grinned. "I'll buy you an apron as a housewarming gift." She could already think of a perfect one: retro, ruffled, black with cherries.

"Don't think I can't rock an apron," Hailey said.

Rachel turned to Cressida. "How are you with it?" she asked. "It'll be a little weird, just the two of us."

Now it was Cressida's turn to redden. "Well, that's what I wanted to talk to you about."

Rachel felt herself stiffen. "Oh?"

"Since Hailey's moving out, and since Noah's moved up here from California..." Cressida cleared her throat. "I was thinking... I want to ask Noah to move in here. With me."

Rachel blinked several times. "Noah? Move in here?"

"I know. It's rushed," Cressida said. "But I've known him for a long time online, and after everything we've been through, I know I love him. I want to be with him."

Rachel swallowed. "It's your house, Cress," she said.

"No, don't be that way," Cressida said quickly. "Just because I bought the house doesn't mean that it isn't still your home, if you want it to be. Both of you," she added, including Hailey.

"I'm making my home with Jake," Hailey said. "But I'll still work at the bookstore every day. And we'll still have girls' night here."

"Will it bother you, Rachel? Having Noah in here, with us?"

Rachel thought about it. It did – but not for the reasons that Cressida might think. She didn't want to be the third wheel, the older sister invading on Cressida's near-connubial bliss. She also saw that Hailey and Cressida were moving on with their lives, much like Stacy was, and Kyla, and Mallory. They had their people.

Meanwhile, Rachel was having sex with Ren and wondering when the whole thing would collapse around her. They were moving forward. She couldn't stop looking back.

"I am happy for you, too," she told Cressida, when she noticed Cressida was anxiously awaiting her response. "I'm surprised, and it is kind of quick, but he seems to really love you, too. And it's not like I was planning on living here forever, either."

"Oh, you don't have to move," Cressida said, looking pained.

"I'll probably wait until after graduation, but it feels like it's time," Rachel said, reassuring her. "And again, it's not like I won't be in here all the time. It's still Frost Fandoms, and we're the Frost sisters."

She pulled them in for a group hug. Hailey sniffled.

"We should've spiked the cocoa," she said. "Damn. I hate being emotional."

"Wait until you're pregnant," Cressida quipped, and Rachel burst into laughter as Hailey glared.

"So what are you doing tonight?" Hailey asked Rachel. "Going back to his place?"

"Yeah," Rachel said, making the decision that moment. "I think I'll..."

Her phone buzzed, and she saw it was a text from Ren. She opened it.

Stuck at the office a little late. Okay for a driver to pick you up, take you to my place? Easier to go from there on a Friday night.

She sighed. Working late, again, this time on a Friday night.

"What is it?" Hailey said perceptively.

Rachel texted Ren back: *Driver's fine. See you at your place.*

"Ren's got to work late," she explained, "so he's sending a driver to pick me up."

"That's got to be nice," Cressida said. "So much more convenient."

"Working late, huh?" Hailey looked suspicious.

"He really is working late," Rachel said. "Of all the things I might worry about with him, cheating on me isn't one of them."

"Of course it isn't." Cressida sounded shocked. "He dumped you, but he was never that guy. The cheating guy."

"He dumped her," Hailey replied. "And they're all potentially that guy."

"It's his family, and the job," Rachel said. "It's his first priority."

They fell quiet as Rachel realized the import of her statement.

I'm not his first priority.

Should she be, though? She frowned at herself. They were just dating. Not even that, to be technical. If she wanted to be his first priority, then maybe she was pursuing the wrong relationship. Maybe she ought to do the smart thing and cut this off now.

"You deserve to be first priority," Cressida said quietly. "I know that much."

"Find you a guy that loves you like a workaholic loves the job," Hailey agreed.

Rachel hugged herself, nodding. "You know what they say most pilots say on the black box, before a plane goes down?"

Hailey looked surprised. "This took a kinda grim turn."

"They say 'oh, shit.' Not screaming or anything, either. Just a sort of resigned, can't do anything about it, oh shit."

Cressida looked at her askance. "Did you hear this on Twitter?"

"I don't remember. Anyway, the point is, I know that Ren and I are a long shot. And I get the feeling there's going to be a point where I just say 'oh, shit' and then call it quits." Rachel raised her chin. "I haven't quite gotten there yet."

"Well, as long as you're optimistic," Cressida said, rolling her eyes. "You might be surprised."

"You're on *his* side, now?" Hailey said.

"No. I'm on Rachel's side, always," Cressida said loyally. "But I also know that if you go in assuming it's going to fail, it's *going to fail.* He cares about you. I'll bet he still loves you."

"It's been ten years," Hailey said. Then she turned to Rachel. "Do you still love him?"

Rachel pressed her lips together. Hailey's jaw dropped. "*No.*"

"I don't know," Rachel said, her voice quiet.

"Well," Cressida said, nudging her, "now might be a good time to figure that out. Give him a chance. A *real* chance."

Rachel felt Cressida's words hit her like a hammer. She'd been analyzing this, kvetching over the possibilities and the pitfalls. Maybe she did need to get out of her own way, and see if this thing with Ren could work.

What was the worst that could happen, right?

You get your heart broken. Again. Worse than last time.

She closed her eyes. She would try some of Cressida's optimism, and hopefully it wouldn't bite her on the ass.

• ♥ • ♥ • ♥ • ♥ • ♥ •

Ren got home exhausted. After his lunch with his parents, the day had been a non-stop revolving door of headaches. He'd implemented a stop gap measure and temporarily put an acting lead engineer in place at the Zhuhai factory, but it was temporary at best. There needed to be better leadership over there. There were also the software issues that still needed to be addressed. He'd finally found the clause that could cancel their contract with the current developer, but that'd be another thing that needed to be replaced and fixed. His muscles felt like they were piano wire, pulled taut as a garrote.

How the hell am I supposed to romance Rachel with all this? He didn't want to go out, especially to some joint that he could grab dinner for less than fifty bucks, and still show her he was thoughtful and romantic. He ought to: she deserved every moment to be special. But God, was he tired.

He heard her knock on his door and winced. He'd have to come up with something. There were some great food trucks over by South Delridge, but that'd probably be cold at this time of year. Still, the food would be excellent. And maybe he could convince her to have it take out, and they could...

What? It's too cold for a picnic. Already took her to the movies. Fancy dinners are out. And just coming back here? Lame.

He let out a sigh as he walked over to the door. He should've come up with something during the day.

When he opened the door, he was surprised to find her with take-out bags in hand already, as well as her backpack with clothes. "Hey there," she said. "I got us pho. That okay?"

He took a deep breath, inhaling the delicious scents of the beef soup. "That sounds just about perfect," he admitted.

"Best part is, we can heat up the broth and eat the soup later," she said, putting stuff down in the kitchen as he closed the door.

He felt a little slow. "Why is that the best part?"

She grinned at him over her shoulder. "Because we don't have to eat right away. How was your day, dear?"

He gave her an answering grin. "Better now."

"Charmer." She tossed her backpack into his room, then took off her coat and tossed it on the bed. Then she studied him. "You look wrung out."

"Thanks." He took off his tie.

"I know you usually do the planning for this dating-fest," she said, walking up to him, "but I thought tonight might be different."

"I'm intrigued." He let her lead him back to the bedroom. He was surprised when she led him to the en suite bathroom.

"It's cold out," she said. "And rainy. And you've had a long, stressful day, and so have I."

"I'm sorry to hear that," he said, stroking her arms.

She smiled at him, then pulled her sweater over her head, leaving her in only a black demi-bra, pushing up the creamy skin of her already pert breasts.

His mouth watered. His palms itched.

"So I was thinking: hot shower," she said, with a sassy smile. "Then soup. It's the perfect thing for a rainy night."

"Sounds absolutely perfect," he growled, his body hardening. He unbuttoned his shirt, cursing at his own clumsiness when he realized his hands were shaking. Watching her slip off her slacks, standing there in black high-cut panties that matched the bra, had him aching. He all but tore his own clothes off.

She slipped out of her bra, then stepped out of her panties, kicking them aside. She turned his shower on, then beckoned him from behind the glass door. "Water's fine," she said, her smile pure sex.

He shoved off his boxers, then joined her in the shower, turning on the other showerhead. She smiled.

"Decadent," she murmured, since water could hit both of them. The shower fogged.

"Handy," he replied. He groaned as the hot water sluiced over him, slowly easing the knots of tension that had collected in between his shoulders, and up his neck. He reached for her, feeling her slick body against his, the water running down in rivulets between them. Down the valley between her breasts, down the flat planes of her stomach. Between the taut muscles of her thighs.

Her hair turned to liquid ebony in the water, and her eyelashes were dotted with crystal water droplets. She blinked at him, her smile wide.

Then she got up on her tiptoes and kissed him, hard.

He opened his mouth, his tongue twining with hers as his cock lodged between their stomachs. She was groaning into him, making these low sexy sounds that made him harder. He wrapped his arms around her, holding her tight against him, her breasts crushed against him, her nipples dragging against his chest. Then he slicked one hand up into her wet hair, tugging her head back so he could devour her neck. He licked at the water before sucking hard, drawing a strangled cry from her. She inched one leg up, anchoring it around his waist.

Oh, hell yeah.

He picked her up, pressing her against the cold tiles. She gasped, and automatically wrapped the other leg around him.

"You are so fucking hot," he said against her skin, sucking a nipple into his mouth and swirling around the nipple with his tongue. She gasped louder, and he heard the thud as she put her head back against the tile. "The things I want to do to this body..."

"Do it," she urged, rolling her hips, arching her back and edging up as if she were trying to climb him.

He reached down with one hand, positioning his cock at her center, which had a wet heat that had nothing to do with the shower. It seduced him. He stroked the head up and down her damp slit, her slickness coating him and almost making him dizzy.

"I want you to fuck me," she murmured in his ear, before nipping at his earlobe. Her fingernails grazed his shoulders. "I want you to fuck me *so hard*, Ren."

He pressed forward, his cock sliding easily, the tip entering...

Then he froze.

"Shit." He rested his head against the tiles behind her shoulder. "Baby, I need to get…"

"Condom?" She moved fractionally, and he moaned at the pleasure that rushed through him.

"Yeah."

"I'm on the pill. I'm clean. I have the records on my phone," she said. "How about you?"

"I'm clean, I've got records," he said, almost stuttering in his haste. "So, you're good with…"

"*Yes*," she said, squirming, her pussy clutching at him.

He didn't need any other encouragement. He drove in, then just about passed out at the sheer, overwhelming pleasure of being inside Rachel naked. He'd never been inside a woman naked before. He was always too careful, too cognizant that someone might want his child, to try and latch onto the Chu empire's riches. But he trusted Rachel.

It made sense that, yet again, she'd be his first.

"Oh, my God," Rachel said, clutching onto him, her thighs holding him tight. He held her in place against the wall as he withdrew, then slid back in, the sensations making them both moan. He kept the pace easy at first, gliding in and out of her. She was so *wet*. "So… *good*…" she whimpered.

He knew what she meant. He'd never felt anything like her wet heat. He started to thrust more insistently, jarring against her as her legs wrapped around him. She reached down, spreading her folds until her clit rubbed against him, then kissed him hard.

The thought of her driving herself towards her pleasure, the feel of her mouth against his, was enough to drive him crazy. He pounded into her against the wall, and she wrapped her arms around him, chanting his name, rolling her hips, meeting his thrusts. He could feel the climax barreling towards him, and he knew that he had to wait.

"You feel so damned good," he told her. "I want to be inside you forever."

"Oh, God, yes." She was bouncing now, her breathing going a million miles an hour. She was getting close, he could feel it. "Keep fucking me. Just like that."

He pounded harder, gripping her ass, pulling her tight against him.

She cried out, a rippling cry of release. *"Ren!"*

He couldn't have held back if he tried. Grunting, gasping, he emptied himself into her, feeling the contractions of her orgasm around the sensitive flesh like it was a fist around his cock.

Don't pass out, was his last cognizant thought for a while. He held her, the water running down on either side of them.

"Feel better?" she asked, and the slim circlet of muscles inside her pussy gripped him playfully for a second.

"When I regain consciousness, I'll let you know," he said, and was gratified by her peal of laughter. "That was amazing."

Slowly, they disengaged themselves, and Ren rubbed at his back. "I'm going to have to work out more to keep up with you," he remarked.

Her eyes sparkled. "That was just round one," she murmured.

Round one? And they didn't have to wear condoms? He suddenly couldn't wait.

They soaped each other up, inadvertently causing him to start getting another erection. "That's going to have to wait until after dinner," she reprimanded, but her eyes were still gleaming.

She was right. The hot shower – and the incredibly hot shower sex – had done wonders to improve his mood. The soup was perfect finishing touch.

"Thank you, again," he said. "You just knew how to take care of me."

She shrugged. "It's no big deal. It's a Friday night – all the restaurants would've been crowded anyway, and it really is miserable out. Besides, it's no hardship."

"What? Having sex with me?" He grinned. "Thanks."

"Taking care of you."

His heart seemed to skip a beat.

"Does that mean you've decided?" he asked quietly. "About us?"

There was a pause, and he felt himself hope.

"Not quite yet," she said, and the hope was squashed. Not entirely, but enough to deflate his ego. "Let's just enjoy this week, okay?"

He frowned. He'd just had amazing shower sex and was probably going to have more sex later. Rachel was here taking care of him. He ought to be happy. But there was something about those words that had him uneasy.

Let's just enjoy this week.

Why did that give him such a sense of doom?

·♥·♥·♥·♥·♥·

Rachel had optimistically brought the marketing strategy textbooks with her, so she could get ahead on her reading that weekend, but Ren was making it difficult. She had taken over his living room, with the books out on his coffee table. He had moved in next to her on the couch, giving her puppy dog eyes, brushing his fingers through her hair, or pressing kisses on her shoulder.

"Ren," she scolded playfully. "I'm trying to read here. I thought you'd have work to do."

He pouted. "I do," he said. "But I'd rather be out here with you."

He nibbled on her earlobe, and she laughed, shivering a little. "We've had sex like four times in the past ten hours," she said.

"I'm making up for lost time." He nuzzled her neck. "Besides, I'm not necessarily trying to have sex with you. I just like being with you. What's that song? The one where the guy says, 'I like me better when I'm with you.' That's how I feel."

She felt her chest warm, like a comfy, cozy fireplace. "I like that you feel that way," she said, nuzzling him back. She sighed. "I feel a little badly. I usually work at the bookstore with Hailey and Cressida on the weekends; it's our busiest time."

He pulled away a little. "Want me to take you there?" he said easily.

And that was exactly what he was like: thoughtful. She could tell he wanted to spend time with her, but if it was important to her, he immediately moved to action. "No, they assured me that they could survive a weekend without my help, and I'll do the books next weekend," Rachel said. "But you'd really take me, huh?"

"Of course."

She smiled, then kissed him gently. "You're a good egg, Ren Chu."

"Don't tell anybody." He kissed her back, just as gently.

"You know, they dropped a few bombs on me yesterday," she said. "That stressful day I told you about? A lot of it was because of them."

"They're giving you a hard time?" he asked.

"No. This was... well, actually, it was good news, it was just unexpected." Rachel bit her lip, remembering the conversation. "Hailey is moving in with her boyfriend, Jake."

"She's moving out of the house, then?" Ren stroked her shoulder absent-mindedly, in slow, small circles. "That's got to be a shock. You three have lived together all these years, right?"

"Yeah. Of course, Hailey's been staying at Jake's for months and months now, so it's not like it's out of the blue. I just think it finally clicked for me how serious the two of them are." She took a deep breath. "What really blindsided me was Cressida's announcement that she's asking her boyfriend of one month to move in with her. Us, I guess."

Now he looked alarmed. "Give me his name," he said, his voice low and deadly serious. "I'll have a background check run. You can't simply have some strange man move into your house."

She smiled. "That's sweet." And she might take him up on it. "But we've known Noah for just over a month now, and Cressida's known him online for over a year. So it's not that I feel unsafe with him moving in. It's just another big change, that's all."

Ren nodded, still looking concerned.

"I think I need to move out." She sighed. "It's funny. I *never* moved out. We couldn't afford the dorms when I got into U Dub, so I stayed at home to cut costs, and then Grandma Frost got sick and it just made more sense to stay put. And then it just got... I don't know. Too easy to stay."

"You got caught up in life," Ren said. "And things just got away from you."

She nodded. "It's time for me to start making my own changes. I'll get my MBA in June, and from there... I don't know. I'll still be a part of the store, I might even still stay with the casino, but I feel like things *need* to change. I need to move on. And the first step is finding my own place to live."

He stared at her, silently, still stroking her shoulder. She finally smiled at him. "What?"

"I know we've only been seeing each other for the past week," he said, "but... well. You could always move in with me."

She goggled at him. "*What?*"

"Too soon?" He laughed, but it sounded a little creaky. "Yeah, that's too soon. And possibly a little creepy."

She thought about it. "I haven't even decided if I want to *date* you again, Ren. And you're suggesting we move in together?"

"I could write up a pros and cons list," he suggested mildly. She giggled. "I'm a pretty good cook."

"That was a decent grilled cheese the other night," she admitted with a smile, humoring him.

"And I have a steady job. I'm good for rent."

"Do you even rent this place?"

"No. That's another pro: I own the place." She could tell he was trying to sound like he was joking – and yet, at the same time, he wasn't. "Although if you wanted to find someplace else, someplace closer to Snoqualmie, we could definitely get something that suited your needs."

He *was* serious.

"I'd make sure that all your shower needs were taken care of," he said, his expression turning smoldering. "And any other needs, come to that."

Her body tightened at the thought. *You've had sex four times. Down, girl!*

"Is there anything else you'd like in a roomie?" he asked.

"Is that what we'd be? Roomies?"

"I prefer the term 'lovers', but we can start with roomies," he said.

She pulled back, staring at him. "Just how serious are you?"

He sighed heavily. "I don't want to scare you. I'm just… putting this out there."

"Why?"

"Because I want you to start thinking of me in your future," he said.

It's too soon! How could he know that he wanted to live with her? Why was he so intent on getting back together with her? How was he so *sure* when she could barely make up her mind?

"You said it yourself: you're going to be making some changes," he clarified. "I want to be part of them."

"We haven't... it's been..." she spluttered, then huffed. "*Why*? How are you so damned *confident* in these decisions?"

His gaze went soft, and his smile was lopsided.

"Because I still love you."

She gaped.

"Yeah. I shouldn't have said that, either," he said, rubbing the back of his neck. "I was going to be a lot cooler about this, believe me. But you *do* something to me. I didn't realize it until I heard your voice again, that I'd been *waiting* to hear your voice for ten years. And then seeing you... God. It was like getting punched right in the gut. I hadn't even realized how much I missed you until then."

She felt the wall around her heart, what little was left, crumble into dust.

"So yeah, I should be cooler about all of this. And I know that you're going to need time, and I don't want to rush or pressure you. But I want you to know: I'm all in on this. I have all these strong feelings – that *you don't need to reciprocate*, especially not yet – and they're not going to go away."

She swallowed as best she could past the lump in her throat.

These were the words she'd always wanted to hear.

She rested her forehead against his, and felt a hot tear crawl down her cheek. He looked at her, then pulled back, stroking the tear away with his thumb.

"I love you, Rachel Frost," he whispered, then kissed her.

She threw her arms around his neck, kissing him back with all the passion she felt for him. He sighed against her, pulling her onto his lap, holding her tight.

They stayed like that, wrapped around each other. It felt like a communion of souls, something more soothing and more tender and more heartfelt than what they'd done previous nights. It wasn't about sex, not in that moment.

It was about love. She could admit it to herself, if only she were brave enough.

She swallowed, hard, then pulled back enough to look into his deep brown eyes.

"I think I still love you, too," she breathed.

His arms around her tightened.

"Then stay with me." His words were like a hammer ringing down on steel. "Keep seeing me. Let's see where this can go."

She closed her eyes. "All right. We'll see how far this goes."

It was like going into freefall. Her stomach dropped, and she felt dizzy and woozy and, frankly, terrified.

So she held him tighter, and prayed that all this would work out.

CHAPTER 10

She loves me.

Ren was up at six, unable to sleep any longer. He felt like a race car filled with nitrous, full of nervous energy and ready to explode. Ever since Rachel's admission on his couch yesterday, he'd been wandering around in a cloud of euphoria. They'd made love tenderly on the couch – *yes, made love, it's official* – after their mutual confession. He'd helped her study a bit, and they'd half-watched *Ready Player One*. He'd even found *The Mummy Returns* on TV, and they'd chuckled through it as they ate some stir fry Rachel had whipped up from the vegetables and meat he'd had in his fridge and freezer. Then he'd carried her to bed, where they'd had sex that was by turns scorching and sweet. She'd fallen asleep naked, the little spoon to his big spoon, and he'd breathed in the scent of her hair and stroked the silk of her skin, and had felt thankful that he'd managed somehow to get her back into his life.

Now, he was making her French toast casserole, one of her favorite breakfasts. He was lucky enough to have a French loaf and some eggs, so he was assembling it and letting it sit for a few hours while she slept. She'd probably think it was ridiculously decadent, but he didn't care. He wanted to spoil her.

His cell phone buzzed on the kitchen counter, and he frowned. It was six in the morning. Who the hell called at six in the morning?

He sighed. It had to be his family. He hoped it wasn't a medical emergency. That said, he somehow doubted it would be.

He answered it on the second ring. "Hello?"

"Ren." It was his father, as he suspected.

"Dad? Are you all right? Is something wrong with Mom?"

"What?" his father asked, disconcerted. "Of course I'm all right. And your mother is fine, she's right here with me."

"Well, it's six o'clock in the morning," Ren said. "I thought it might be urgent."

His father coughed. "Right. We were just about to get on the plane and head back to Seattle. I forgot about the time difference."

His parents barely seemed to need sleep. His father ran on pure adrenaline, it seemed. His mother supplemented it with high grade coffee and willpower.

"We need to talk to you," his father said. "We talked with the factory last night."

"It was Saturday," Ren said, then realized there was no point. "What did you decide?"

"You're going to need to go to Zhuhai."

"We discussed this," Ren reminded him. He thought of Rachel in his bed. It was a long flight to China. He'd never entertained the idea of joining the Mile-High club, but with Rachel...

"For about two years, we're thinking," his father added.

Ren froze. "Wait. *What?*"

"I'm also thinking of establishing you as Chief Operating Officer, and replacing Peter," his father said. "Your mother and I discussed it, and we think you're ready. You've made good decisions, and there's no reason we can't move leadership for the Electronics Division to Zhuhai."

"But Dad..."

"There's a software developer in Macau that could replace the one we're using," his father kept going, rolling over Ren's protests. "That kills two birds with one stone. Jian can handle the American operations as your right-hand man."

"Dad!"

His father finally paused. "What?"

"You're talking about me moving completely out of the States," he said slowly. "You're talking about uprooting my whole *life*."

His father sighed. "This isn't about that girl, is it?"

You're goddamned right it's about "that girl," Dad!

Ren gritted his teeth. "She's part of it, yes."

"You know that we need to take swift action on this," his father said, in a firm voice. "You also must realize that this is not a whim. This is the next logical step."

The damned thing was, it *did* make sense. And if Rachel wasn't in his life, he'd do it without blinking. It would annoy him, but it wouldn't occur to him to question it.

But Rachel *was* in his life now. He felt a trembling sense of panic skitter at the edges of his nerve endings. How was she going to take this kind of news?

"We'll discuss it more tomorrow, at the office," his father said, and it was like a king making a final decree. There was no room for discussion. Just like Jian's reassignment and Meili's transfer, these were marching orders. As a good family foot soldier, he was expected to comply.

He felt a wrenching sense of loss.

"There's got to be another way to do this," Ren said.

"What?"

"I mean, I don't have to move all the way over there." His mind was whirring with possibilities. There had to be a way to escape this trap. "I'll put in extra time here, and we can get someone in place there, a liaison, that can manage the factory. And there are plenty of developers here that we can work with – Seattle's crawling with them. There have got to be other options than me moving across the ocean."

His father went silent for a long fraught moment. Then he let out a breath.

"Ren," he said quietly. "This is not up for discussion."

Ren felt his heart sink.

"Your mother wants to talk to you," his father said, and Ren heard the phone shuffle from one hand to another.

"Ren?" his mother said. "I was afraid you'd take the news like this, which is why I thought we should tell you as soon as possible. I told him we should have called you last night."

He was oddly glad that they hadn't, since it would've cut his happy evening with Rachel short. He thought of Rachel's words: *let's just enjoy this week.*

Like she'd seen this coming.

"Mom," he said slowly, "this is too sudden a decision. We need to talk about it."

"I know you care about Rachel," she said, in her best let's-be-reasonable voice, "but you haven't seen her for years. In those years, you've been working towards taking over the company. We need to know you're responsible. We *need* you to go to Zhuhai."

He gripped the granite countertop. "I've done everything you've asked. For the past ten years. I got top grades at school, I've done the internships, I've made the targets and whipped the divisions into shape," he said, and his voice was rough.

"What, do you want congratulations?" she asked, and her voice went whip-sharp. "Jian and Meili also got top grades, just as your father and I did when we were your age. In this world, you have to be competitive. No one is going to applaud you for doing your job! Or feel sorry for you when you're given an assignment you don't like!"

Ren felt the sting of her disapproval like a slap across the face.

"You know what you need to do," she said. "You know what's best for the company. And you're going to *do* what is best for the company, without arguing about it, or you're no longer going to be *part* of the company."

Or our family.

It wasn't stated. It didn't need to be.

Ren felt his stomach knot.

"The plane is about to take off," his mother said. "We will discuss the particulars tomorrow, in the office, as your father said. So if there's anything you need to take care of, do it this weekend."

Translation: if you're worried about Rachel, handle it today. Because after tomorrow, we're packing your bags and shipping you off.

"How much time do I have?"

"We want you out there before the end of March," his mother said. "Ideally, in the next two weeks. I've already looked into getting you a condo there, and your office will be set up by the end of the week."

Two weeks.

"Tomorrow morning," she said. "Nine a.m. We'll see you in the office."

With that, she hung up.

Ren stared at the phone, then put it down gingerly on the counter.

Moving to Zhuhai in two weeks.

He knew there would be paperwork, visas, a mess of things to handle. But he also knew that the Chu corporation had people who handled just such paperwork nightmares. He'd be on a plane with a few full suitcases in a few weeks.

And what did that mean for Rachel?

He closed his eyes.

How can I lose her again?

· ♥ · ♥ · ♥ · ♥ · ♥ ·

Rachel woke up and stretched, feeling deliciously sore and a little turned on. It had been years since she'd felt like this. It was still fragile, but she was floating on a cloud of happiness. She'd admitted she loved Ren, and was willing to take a chance on him. On *them*.

It was still scary, but for the first time in a long time, she felt hope.

She was surprised that Ren wasn't still in bed with her. She hoped he wasn't working. That was going to be a bone of contention between them, she could already tell. He worked too hard, and she wasn't sure if it was worth it. She'd worked hard, but always with an end goal in mind.

His end goal always seemed to be "keep my parents happy" and she wasn't sure if that was ever going to be possible.

She pulled on a T-shirt and panties, and wandered out of the bedroom. Something smelled delicious, so she headed for the kitchen first. There was a freshly baked French toast casserole sitting in its pan on the counter, and her stomach yowled in gratitude. She laughed, then went hunting for Ren.

She found him sitting in his home office, frowning at his laptop. "You made breakfast," she said, her voice husky. "And my favorite, too."

He looked at her, and she was momentarily taken aback by the pain she saw in his eyes. He reached for her, and she stepped into his embrace without hesitation. He rested his head against her breasts, holding her tight.

"Hey," she said, nudging his head up so she could study him. "Are you okay? What's up?"

"Work stuff. It can wait." He kissed her stomach, then stood up and kissed her on the forehead, the tip of her nose, and her mouth. "I love you."

She felt the words tingle through her, right to her toes. "I love you, too," she said softly.

He stroked her hair, holding her against his chest. She nuzzled into him, her arms around his waist. They stood there quietly for a long moment. She felt cherished, she realized. He treated her like she was precious to him. She'd waited so long for that feeling.

Finally, he kissed the top of her head. "Come on, let's eat."

"You should definitely carb up," she said, wiggling her eyebrows as he took her hand and led her to the kitchen. "I've got big plans for you, and you're going to need energy to burn."

He didn't laugh, just gave her a half-hearted smile.

Her heart started beating a little faster, and it had nothing to do with her innuendo. *Work, my ass. Something is wrong.*

She frowned. She needed to find out what it was. If they were going to be in a relationship – and she'd told him they would be – then he couldn't keep bottling up emotions. She was a grown ass woman. She could handle whatever he could dish out.

Breakfast was subdued. She wanted to enjoy the custardy bread, but she found herself having a hard time swallowing. Irritation grew inside her as she saw him getting more and more morose.

"Okay, *what is it?*" she burst out. "You're acting like somebody you love got shot. What the hell happened between last night and this morning that has you so upset?"

"I told you. Work thing."

"What work thing?" She frowned. "I know I'm not an MBA yet, but I think I can follow along."

He looked at her, and the pain in his gaze magnified. It was written all over his face now.

The bubble of fear in her chest grew, as well.

"My parents called this morning. Stupid early, six a. m.," he said. "You were still asleep, and I was making breakfast. Anyway, we've been having problems with this factory... I told you about that."

"Okay. Are they blaming you for the problems?" Rachel asked.

"No. They know what the problems are. It's a leadership thing. They need the COO to handle some process stuff better. They need a new lead engineer, they need a new software developer, they need a bunch of problems solved and fixed, and then they need sales to rebound because we show the customers that the problems have been fixed."

"Well, that sounds like a pain," Rachel admitted. "But it also sounds like nothing new for you. You've been working on all these things, right? And you're putting in long hours. Are they upset with you because things aren't fixed yet?"

"Yes," Ren said slowly. "But again, that's not quite the problem."

Rachel's eyes narrowed. "Is it me?" She paused. "That seems really egotistical, to think that this has to do with me, but they never really liked me. I think they saw me as a distraction."

Ren grimaced, and Rachel felt her stomach knot. "They do still see you as a bit of a distraction, but that doesn't matter," Ren said. "I told them I want to be with you, no matter what."

Rachel let out a strained breath. "I want to be with you, too."

"No matter what?" Ren asked, with particular urgency.

She felt that niggle of fear again, the bubble growing bigger, pressing at her rib cage. "What happened, Ren?"

He looked trapped, she realized. She ran his fingers through his hair, one of his nervous habits. One he hadn't done since she'd seen him again. He was so composed now, seeing him shaken was starting to freak her out.

"They want me to take over as COO," he said slowly. "And... they want me to move to Zhuhai and lead the team from there."

She blinked. "They want you to move to China?"

He nodded. "For two years," he added. "At least."

It was like getting run over by a truck. She felt stunned, and a hard press of pain as the fear bubble burst.

He's leaving.

He quickly moved to her side. "I know what you're thinking," he pleaded. "And I know, the timing absolutely sucks..."

"You think?" She let out a small, hysterical laugh.

"We just found each other again, and now I'm supposed to go half a world away," he said. "But I think we can make this work."

"*How*? How do you think we can make this work?" Rachel felt her eyes start to sting with tears. Damn it, she knew, she *knew* she shouldn't have trusted this.

She was important – until she wasn't. Until something with a higher priority came along. His job and his place in Chu Enterprises would always take precedent.

"I have an idea," he said, and his voice was coaxing as he stroked her back, trying to soothe her. "It'll be challenging, but I think it might be good."

She closed her eyes. What was he thinking? Flying back once a month? Regular sexting via Skype? Of course, that was when his work permitted...

She knew she was being bitter. She felt she had a right. She'd set herself up for this one, so she was angry with herself, as well.

"I want you to come with me."

That stopped her mental loop in its tracks. "What?" she croaked.

"Move with me. To Zhuhai." His eyes shone with sincerity. "Long distance is too hard, and I want you with me. So why not come with me?"

Her mouth fell open. "Come with you?" she repeated. "To China?"

She waited for him to tell her it was just a joke, no big deal. Instead, he was looking at her with complete solemnity.

"Come with me," he repeated, and took her hand.

Ren saw the shock on Rachel's face as he asked the question. He'd thought about it for the past three hours. It seemed crazy, but really, was it that much crazier than simply asking her to move in with her?

Yes, it totally is.

He shrugged off his conscience. He was going to make this work, one way or another. He was *not* going to lose Rachel again. And if that meant getting the visa department to work on two sets of paperwork rather than one, well, that's what was going to happen.

Rachel stared at him, pulling her hand out of his grasp. "You want me to move with you? To Zhuhai?" Her eyes were wide and startled. "When?"

This was another tricky part. "Well, they want me to move kind of quickly..."

"*How* quickly?"

"Two weeks." He grimaced when she seemed to pull even further away, pushing herself against the back of the dining room chair. "That doesn't mean you'd have to leave that soon. I'd take care of all the arrangements."

"I'm still in school!"

Did that mean she was thinking about it? He leaned forward, pressing his advantage. "You could finish school. They might even let you finish it remotely," he added, thinking that Chu Enterprises could donate a building or something if that could happen.

Okay, you're thinking a little crazy now.

"You'd love Zhuhai," he wheedled. "It's beautiful. Palm trees, theme parks, golf courses... and it's right by Macau. That's like the Las Vegas of Asia."

"I already work in a casino," she said, her tone acidic. "It's not like casinos have a special magic for me, remember? And what do you think I'd be doing over there? I don't speak the language. I wouldn't know anybody!"

"You'd know me. We'd be together."

Her eyes were wheeling now. "I'd be isolated. I'd be something like seven thousand miles away from my family and friends!"

"About sixty-five hundred," he said. "And I'd make sure you could fly back often."

She kept staring at him. Then she laughed, a bitter, harsh sound.

"You really think this is going to work, don't you?"

"I want it to," he said. "More than anything."

She looked down at the table, at her empty plate. Then she got up, mechanically grabbing the dirty dishes and taking them to the sink. He followed her, unnerved by her intense silence.

"What are you thinking?" he asked finally, after watching her rinse the dishes and put them in the washer. "Don't shut me out."

"I'm thinking about ten years ago."

He let out a harsh sigh. "This is different."

"You know, it really isn't." She looked at him, and her violet eyes were clouded with pain. "I thought I was going to marry you. I would've done anything for you. Including a long-distance relationship. I even considered walking away from U Dub and following you to Boston." She shook her head. "But you couldn't... no. You *didn't want* to make that work."

"I let my parents get in my head," he said, but it felt like an excuse as soon as it came out of his mouth. "I was a stupid kid. I was just eighteen. *This is different.*"

"Let's look at this logically." Her voice was steady, even though her expression wasn't. "Your job is just like school: it's too important to ignore, and you've got your family pressuring you to excel. You can't afford to screw this up."

"I need you with me."

Her beautiful face was frozen in a look of pity. "Tell me, Ren. Is that what *I* need?"

"We're better together," he argued. "We love each other!"

"I love my family, too. And my friends. They've been here for me. I love the area, the Pacific Northwest... Snoqualmie and Seattle, and everything in between. I love the life I've carved out here." He saw tears start to well up in her eyes, and it stabbed him in the chest. "I know things are changing, but I am not going to move out to China simply because I don't want to be alone when everybody else is pairing up. And I'm not going to rip up my whole life just because the guy I'm in love with has an unhealthy job and he wants to drag me along with him."

He felt her words slamming into him like bullets. "I'm not trying to..."

Then he stopped.

That was *exactly* what he was trying to do.

"It could be an adventure," he said, but it felt weak. "But you're right. I have no right to ask you to move to China with me. You're too invested here, and it's not fair to upend your life because mine is."

She nodded.

"But we could make the long-distance work, if you're open to it," he said, shifting gears. He was *not* going to lose her. "I've got a private plane, for God's sake. I could fly back every other weekend. I could fly you out other weekends. We could talk every night..."

She was already shaking her head, and he felt desperation claw at him.

"What? Why would that not work?"

"I love you," she said, and cradled his face with her hand. "But we both know what's wrong with that scenario."

"I don't."

She took a deep breath. "You're going to be too busy for me," she pointed out. "This is really important to your family, and important to you, and you can't afford to be distracted."

He winced. Those were almost the exact words he'd used to break up with her.

"See? It's the same thing as before, just on a ten-year delay." She shook her head.

"I'm different now, damn it." He held her by her shoulders. "I don't want to lose you!"

"I'm different, too." Her eyes flashed. "And I'm *not* going to do this, do you understand? You were the one who pursued me. You were the one who said it'd be different this time. Now you're asking me to put my life on hold and take whatever time you can allot when you're not too busy, and you know what? *Fuck that*, Ren. I deserve better than this!"

Her chest was heaving, she was breathing so hard. Tears tumbled down her cheeks. He pulled her to him, and she shoved him away.

"Don't... just don't." She swiped the tears away with the back of her hand. "I'm leaving. We're done."

The words were like the ringing of a nail in his coffin. He watched as she stormed back to the bedroom, changing out of his T-shirt, into regular clothes. He waited, his mind racing, trying to come up with some reason she should stay that wasn't completely, utterly selfish.

He couldn't think of a single thing.

She came out, bag slung over her shoulder. She looked at him. "I called an Uber. It'll be downstairs in a minute." Her eyes were red.

"Rachel..."

"Don't call me, Ren. Don't get in contact with me again."

He grimaced. "Just like last time."

"Yeah, I should've made that stick." She bit her lip. "Goodbye, Ren."

Everything in his being was screaming at him to stop her, somehow. Fix this. Get her to change her mind. But he loved her, and he knew: this was the wrong thing for her. He had no right.

"Goodbye, Rachel," he said, and watched her walk out the door.

CHAPTER 11

Rachel cried enough in the Uber that the driver, a woman, asked if she was okay.

"Just broke up with my boyfriend," Rachel said, wiping at the tears that continued to fall and then digging around in her backpack for her package of tissues.

"There are tissues in the seatback," the driver offered helpfully. "I'm so sorry you're going through this."

Thankfully, the woman was not talkative enough to want to discuss it, or trade breakup horror stories. She did change the channel from a radio station playing an Ed Sheeran love song to NPR, for which Rachel was thankful. She didn't think she could handle hearing about how perfect a woman was for him. Right now, she just wanted to either throat punch someone, or curl up in a ball and weep.

She got to the bookstore, and winced at the price for the ride, but thanked the driver. Slinging her backpack over one shoulder, she headed up the steps. The store was still open, and there were people milling around, browsing. Cressida was ringing someone up at the cash register when she got a look at Rachel.

"Hailey," Cressida called quietly.

Hailey emerged from the other room. "What's..."

Then Hailey got a look at Rachel, and turned a brilliant red. She rushed to Rachel's side.

"What happened? What did he do?" she hissed, dragging Rachel back into the kitchen, away from the customers. "I swear, I will *gut* that fucking..."

"We broke up, that's all." Rachel sniffled, grabbing a napkin and mopping at her eyes, her nose.

"He *dumped* you? Again?"

"No. I dumped him this time."

Hailey harrumphed. "Well, that's something, at least." She calmed slightly. "What happened?"

Rachel sighed, then the story came out, in bits and pieces. How she'd finally told him she loved him, and that she was willing to give him a chance. Then his parents' call, and the shocking reveal that he was moving to China in two weeks.

"And he asked you to go with him?" Hailey said, sounding as stunned as she looked. "What is he, high?"

Rachel laughed, a high-pitched, nervous sound. "I know. It felt insane when he was pitching me on it."

Cressida came back to the kitchen. "I caught enough of what happened," she said, looking in the front room to ensure there weren't customers who needed attention. "Are you staying here because of us, Rachel?"

Rachel turned to her sister, startled. "What do you mean?"

"It could be a grand adventure," she said, sounding sad. "And I feel like, sometimes, you put so much on hold because of what *our* family needed. Taking care of Grandma. Staying here to make sure we had enough to pay rent. I know," Cressida said, holding her hands up defensively when Rachel started to protest. "You wanted to make these choices, and you're a grown woman. But I want to make sure that you're not giving up Ren because of us."

"I promise you," Rachel said vehemently, "it wasn't that. I made this choice for *me*. I am tired of coming in second, to college, to work."

"Do you feel like he's making you choose between your family and him?"

"You guys really didn't come into it," she admitted. "But if he'd asked me to choose between you guys and him, I'd obviously choose you guys."

"Why?"

"Because I love you." Rachel stared at Cressida, wondering what her point was. "And because you'd never ask me to make that kind of choice. Hell, Hailey never trusted

Ren, but she still backed my play when I continued to see him."

"And look how well that turned out," Hailey grumbled.

Cressida looked thoughtful. "I think he's trying to choose between his family and you," she said slowly. "And he doesn't know how."

Rachel frowned. They were the pressure behind him taking the job. Was she trying to make him choose?

No. She had chosen herself. She knew what she wanted, and what she deserved. What he did from there was up to him.

"I can't help him there," Rachel said, slow and thoughtful. "I don't even think he likes his job. He is trying to prove himself, trying to jump through all these hoops. And the hoops keep getting higher. And lit on fire." She shook her head. "But that's his problem. Not mine. I'm not going to move to Macau with him just because he's going to keep jumping."

Hailey put an arm around her shoulder. "Putting it that way, I feel a little – just a *tiny little* – bit sorry for the guy," she admitted. "But you're my sister, and I love you. So if he can't get it together, then the hell with him."

Rachel smiled. "Thanks, Hailey."

"Want me to see if we can pull together a girls' night?" Cressida said. "I'll activate the phone tree."

"Oh, no, I don't need..."

"Nonsense," Cressida said matter-of-factly. "You didn't get to have a full support session when you guys broke up in high school. You're long overdue."

Rachel shrugged. "Okay. Why not?"

· ♥ · ♥ · ♥ · ♥ · ♥ ·

Ren showed up at his father's office at nine a.m. the following morning, per their email. He'd been up most of the night. Ever since Rachel had left his home, he'd been in a state of... how to describe it? Shock? Depression? Anger?

How about all of the above?

He didn't blame Rachel for leaving. She was right. She deserved better than a half-assed proposition that was just trying to keep everybody in his life placated. He did want to live with her, but that didn't mean he wanted to drag her across the world against her wishes. He did want to show her that she was special in his life.

He'd done a piss-poor job of that beyond a couple of dinners and a movie. He rubbed at the back of his neck, the tension straining to the point where he felt like his skull was fused onto his shoulders.

He was beyond exhausted, and realized that he had been for some time. Possibly for years. He needed to finally address it.

He nodded to his father's assistant and walked into the large office where they were waiting. His mother looked at him with a small, satisfied smile. "Good, you're on time. We have a lot to go over."

His father had some folders and packets of papers spread out on his desk. "The first issue is the visa, but that shouldn't be a problem. We've…"

"I need to talk to the two of you," Ren interrupted.

His mother's smile slipped into an expression of irritation, and she glanced at her husband. "I told you," she said quietly.

His father crossed his arms, his eyes narrowed and angry. "We are not discussing alternatives," he said, in a sharp voice. "We aren't going to discuss how you could work from here. We've already decided on this course of action, and it's not getting any more attention. Is that clear?"

"I'm not moving to Zhuhai."

The bald pronouncement had his parents shocked silent for a second. Then his father's chested puffed. "What do you mean, you're not moving there?"

"Just that. I'm not moving to Zhuhai. I'm staying here, in Seattle."

"That is not an option," his mother said.

"It is if I quit."

If he'd shocked them before, he downright galvanized them now.

"You're quitting?" his father asked, jaw slightly agape.

"You're bluffing," his mother responded, but she looked shaken. "You're our oldest son, the heir to the chairmanship. You know that. You've worked every day of your life towards that goal. Now, you're going to throw a temper tantrum, and quit, all because of some... some *girl*?"

"It's not because of some girl," he said. "Rachel plays into it, I'm not going to deny that. But damn it, I work eighty to hundred-hour weeks here. I don't have a life. And we *encourage* that." He shook his head. "If I had a wife, any wife, I don't know how she'd be okay with that. And if she was, I don't know that *I'd* be okay with her being okay with it."

"There are women here at the company..." his mother pointed out, and he stopped her.

"That's not the point, Mom. The point is, I haven't been happy for a long time. I just didn't think about it. It was all laid out for me: that I was going to be chairman of the board and CEO and all this stuff. And I *don't even want it*. Not if it means I don't have any life of my own!"

His mother stared at him as if he'd grown two heads. Then her expression turned cold.

"So you're going to turn your back on everything we've done for you. We worked this hard to build this company up to what it is, and you're spitting on it."

He felt his chest clench, and he grimaced. "I love you, and I appreciate everything you've done for me. But what you want isn't what I want."

"Then I suppose you'll be all right turning your back on everything. Because if you walk out of here, you're no son of ours." She raised her chin up, her eyes bright. "Out of the will. Cut off from everything. Is that what you want?"

"I told you, I love you," Ren said. "Both of you. But I'm not going to be held emotionally and financially hostage here. If you want to cut me off, do what you think is best. But I'm done. I can't do this anymore."

It was not the answer she was expecting, judging by the crestfallen expression on her face. His father had turned red, anger obviously at the fore, mixed in liberally with disappointment.

"You're going to be sorry you made this decision," his father said, his words clipped.

Ren swallowed hard. "I'm sorry I didn't make the decision sooner," he said.

His father picked up his phone. "Yes. Please send security up here," he said. "I want them to accompany Ren Chu to his desk to be emptied, then I want them to escort him out of the building."

"Dad," Ren said.

His father hung up the phone with a slam. "Get out. *Now.*"

Ren nodded, feeling the pain. He'd apparently just been disowned. He knew it would come to this point. But at the same time, there was a weird sense of lightness. Of *freedom*.

No more late nights and pointless meetings. No more sense of falling short. No more feigning interest in a company he was feeling more and more distanced from. He'd never even thought about whether or not he liked what he was doing until he reconnected with Rachel. Now he realized: there were a million things he *could* be doing out there.

One of them was being happy.

He emptied his desk under the surprised eyes of Jose and Frank, two security guards he'd known since he started working in the building. "We're really sorry about this, Mr. Chu," Jose said.

"No big deal," he said, as they walked him to the elevator. Before he got there, Jian accosted him.

"*Are you out of your fucking mind?* You *quit*?" Jian looked like someone had hit him in the back of the head with a two-by-four, his eyes bugging out. "What the hell happened?"

"They told me they wanted me to move to Zhuhai in two weeks," he said. "And they wanted me to move for two years."

Jian let out a low whistle. "Well, that does kinda suck," he admitted. "But... quitting?"

"They weren't open to any other options. And you know what? I'm okay with it."

"What are you going to do now?"

"I've got savings to fall back on," Ren said. "I also bought a few houses, a few years ago, and the rentals have been decent. I mean, I'm not going to be living opulently, but it should carry me until I get another job. And I may just take a break. I've been running kinda ragged for the past few years."

"Welcome to Chu Enterprises," Jian said bitterly. "Man. Now all your shit's going to fall on me."

"It doesn't have to," Ren pointed out. He sighed. "They're probably not going to want you to talk to me for a while. They won't be talking to me." His parents were champion grudge-carriers. He hoped that they could get to some peaceful spot, but he felt sadness that it might not be for a long time.

"Meili and I will work on them," Jian said. "And you're my brother. I've got your back."

He gave Jian an awkward half-hug, still holding his file box of stuff from his desk: a few photos, some books, things from his desk. "I'll talk to you soon, then."

He went down to his car, putting the file box in the trunk. His next step: talk to Rachel. She'd told him she didn't want him to contact her ever again, and he wanted to honor that. But he also knew that he wanted to have one last chance, one last try. If she shut him out from there, so be it. But they both deserved to find out what would happen now that his life had changed so radically. Now that he could finally put her first.

He only prayed that he wasn't too late in his realization.

Rachel sat in her bedroom that evening, even though the bookstore was still open. She had a paper to start working on, so she had her laptop out on her desk. Unfortunately, her scene with Ren the previous day was still preying on her. He'd tried calling her today, and texted her several times that he needed to talk to her, but she quickly shut her phone off. She'd probably block his number.

Her heart hurt. It had only been a week that they were back together, as it were, and she felt like all the old scars had been torn open. She curled up on her bed, watching Netflix on her iPad and trying like hell to live in someone else's world for a few hours.

She'd barely slept, and she'd considered calling in sick to work, but she didn't. She didn't want to put that much emphasis on Ren in her life. Also, her sisters were treating her like a fragile flower already – she didn't want to feed that particular instinct.

You got over him before. You'll get over him now.

And it was different now, because she felt like she'd stood up for herself. She deserved better, and she wasn't going to give up her life because some guy had more important things that needed to be accommodated.

Even if that guy is Ren.

She frowned. She had her headphones in, but she swore she heard yelling. Pulling out her earbuds, she heard a man's voice. "RACHEL! RACHEL!"

Was that... it couldn't be Ren.

Could it?

What the hell was he doing here? And why was he yelling?

She rushed out of her bedroom and down the three flights of stairs. She could hear Hailey's sharp voice.

"You're going to get out of here, *now*, or I'm calling the cops!" Hailey growled.

"I know she doesn't want to talk to me," Ren said back. "But there's something she needs to know before she makes the decision to cut me out of her life."

"I think she already knows!" Hailey snapped. "You think that you're more important than her, that your needs are more important. *Like right now!* What she needs is for you to *leave her the fuck alone!*"

Rachel came around the corner in time to see him wince. The customers were getting an eyeful tonight, apparently.

"I know, it's not fair. And I wouldn't have come here if there were any other way," Ren said. "But I took what she said seriously..."

"Apparently not the bit about not contacting me," Rachel interjected.

He looked over at her, and she couldn't help it – her heart squeezed. She felt like she couldn't breathe. He looked at her like she was some kind of radiant light, some holy object.

"Rachel," he breathed, taking a step closer to her.

Hailey jumped in his way. "Cress, call..."

"No, it's okay," Rachel said. "I want to hear what it is that is so important, it overrides my express desire not to have contact."

He looked pained. "I am so sorry," he said.

"Not good enough. Get out."

"Not sorry about yesterday... I mean, I'm sorry about that, too," he said quickly. "But I'm sorry I came over. I just didn't want you to leave without knowing..."

"Knowing what?"

"That I quit my job."

She gasped. "You *what*?"

"I quit. I'm no longer with Chu Enterprises." He looked relieved at the announcement. He took another step towards her. "I'm not moving to Zhuhai, or anywhere else."

Rachel felt confused. "You didn't quit for me, did you?"

"Not just for you," he said. "You were right. It was unhealthy, a complete shit show, and when they pushed me to relocate without hearing any other alternatives, I realized it was always going to be that way. And that I didn't want that in my life." He was quiet for a second, then his voice turned hoarse. "I want *you* in my life."

Her chest grew warmer, like a thousand embers were glowing there. She felt her eyes well up with tears.

"I love you, Rachel," he said. "I understand this is a lot, and again, I'm sorry I broke my word and came over here. But I'm also not sorry, if it gives us a chance. If you need time to think about it, I'll understand. And if you just want me to turn around and never come back, I swear I'll respect it. But I'm honestly hoping that you'll be able to forgive me, and give me that second chance."

"Third chance," she corrected, her voice sounding a little watery. She felt a tear emerge, crawling down her cheek.

"However many chances you're willing to give me." Ren studied her carefully. "I never want to hurt you. I'm sorry I was such an asshole, putting you on the spot, not thinking of your needs."

She took a deep breath, staring back at him. He was wearing a T-shirt and jeans, not his usual suit. His hair looked like he'd run his fingers through it frantically, probably most of the day. She thought about his calls.

"Come up with me," she said, "and we'll talk."

She tugged him away from Hailey and the customers, bringing him back to her room and closing the door. He looked wary, and full of longing.

She could understand both of those feelings.

"So you quit." She sat on the bed, watching him. "How'd that go?"

"They're really, really pissed." He let out a low, ragged laugh. "And I've been disowned."

She felt a pang. "I didn't want to tear you away from your family."

"They wouldn't accept anything less than complete compliance. And I just don't have that to give anymore." He looked at her, questioning, and gestured next to her on the bed, as if asking for permission. She nodded, and he sat down next to her gingerly, still staring at her. "I didn't want to have to make that choice, but it was mine to make. You didn't push me into it. You just showed me how badly I was living. And you were right: you deserved better."

He raised his hand, like he was going to stroke her cheek, or her shoulder. Then he carefully put it back down.

"I want to give you everything you deserve," he said, his voice solemn. "I love you, Rachel. I'll always love you. I want to make this work, but it's all in your court now. I'll do whatever you say."

Rachel's head was spinning. He'd never stood up to his family before. He'd certainly never put her before something as outwardly important as school or work.

He'd chosen *her*. And he was giving her the reins, letting her decide whether or not they continued.

She swayed towards him, resting her head on his chest, and his arms wrapped around her.

"Rachel," he breathed. "I'm so sorry. I love you."

"I love you, too," she admitted, and felt his arms squeeze tighter. She tugged away, turning to look him in the face. "Don't ever hurt me like that again."

"I won't. I promise." He leaned down, kissing her tear away, stroking her hair.

"Maybe we'll take it slow," she said.

"Whatever speed you need," he agreed. "I told you before, I'd wait. We'll make this work."

She curled against him. Then she leaned up, brushing a kiss against his mouth. It tasted sweeter than their others – more tender, more *real*.

She trusted him. He'd made his choice, and he'd chosen her. It felt unbelievable, and at the same time, unmistakable.

"Maybe we won't take it slow," she said, then kissed him with a little more hunger, a little more intent.

He groaned against her lips. "Anything," he said, "for you."

EPILOGUE

It was a fortunate sunny day in Seattle, and Rachel stood in her cap and gown in line, just waiting for…

"Rachel Frost!"

Rachel stepped up to the podium, accepting her diploma with a handshake, and felt her heart soar.

Her MBA. She'd worked her ass off for this for the past three years. Now, it felt like she was free, and like the world was opening up to her like a picture book, full of options and color and *life*.

She looked back into the crowds, where she could see her family and friends cheering her on. Hailey had her phone up, and was no doubt video-relaying it all back to Cressida and Noah at the bookstore. The women from girls' night were all out in force, clapping and whistling, all with their respective boyfriends.

And there was Ren, who was smiling broadly and applauding like she'd won the Nobel prize.

They'd been inseparable for the past four months. He had taken a month off to just "decompress" and figure out what he wanted. She was still living at the bookstore, since it was still so much closer to work. But he'd stayed the night during the week, making or buying her meals, doing dishes, and generally helping out around the house. Thankfully, he'd slowly won Hailey over with his devotion.

Now, he was working as a COO for a company in Seattle. It was a smaller, family-run business, one that made marine parts for ships. He wasn't making nearly his salary at Chu, but it was still decent, and as he said, "I get to have my time and my soul back." He made sure he had weekends off and got home at a decent hour, something his boss insisted on for all employees.

After the ceremony, Rachel walked to her friends and family, who cheered and pulled her into a group embrace. "You did it!" Kyla said, with another hug.

"Grandma Frost would be so proud of you," Hailey said, looking emotional. Then she cleared her throat, waving at her eyes. "I am *not* going to start crying!"

Everyone laughed at that. Hailey, tough-as-nails Hailey, was not the type to burst into tears.

"Okay, Cressida's holding down the fort in Snoqualmie, so what say we head back and start that graduation party?" Mallory said, with a smile.

There was another set of cheers. Rachel put a hand on Ren's arm, holding him back. "We'll be right behind you!" she called to the disappearing crowd. Then she pulled him aside.

He looked puzzled. "You all right?"

"I just can't believe this year," she said. "The things that have happened to all of us. Cressida's kicking ass with the bookstore, and Hailey's going to Australia with Jake for a *Mystics* convention there, and now I've got my MBA."

"It's been a lot," he agreed. "I changed jobs – and I got back together with you."

He'd been so careful. He hadn't pressured her about them moving in together. He'd let her set the pace for all their interactions. He was trying to make it up to her, trying to keep her in the driver's seat.

"I'm moving out of the bookstore."

He froze. "Oh?" She could tell from his expression that he wanted to put in a request, but he didn't. "Have any ideas where you'd be moving to?"

"I don't exactly," she said. "But I'm thinking of looking for a job in the city. I'll still work at the bookstore in an administrative capacity, but Hailey and Cressida have the rest locked down – they don't really need me. And I think I've outgrown the casino."

"So, you're thinking Seattle."

She could see how hard he was biting his tongue. She was amazed at his restraint.

"Ren," she finally said gently, "you can ask."

"Would you consider moving in with me?" The words tumbled out in a rush. "It's only been four months, I know, but..."

"It's been four great months," she said, and he put his arms around her, kissing her forehead. "I was thinking of something else, though."

He stared into her eyes. "Yes?"

"I know how careful you've been, and I love that," she said. "But you don't need to keep walking on eggshells with me. I know you're committed. I know just how important you think I am."

"I've tried every day to show that," he said.

"So I was thinking..." And now her throat burned, and her stomach jittered with nerves, "maybe we could take this to the next level."

He tilted his head, uncomprehending.

"I'm committed to you, too," she said. "And I never stopped loving you. We might've been too young, but I think we ultimately knew what we wanted, and where we belonged."

He stared at her, then it was like Christmas and New Year's and the Fourth of July, all rolled into one. "You mean..."

"We could consider it," she whispered. "Unless..."

He reached into his suit coat pocket, producing a velvet box. Her jaw dropped as he got down on one knee, opening the box to reveal a diamond engagement ring.

It was oval cut, not too flashy. Elegant and beautiful. Just what she loved.

"Rachel," he said, his breathing harsh. "Would you marry me?"

She raised her hands to her mouth. "Holy shit," she said. "Were you going to propose today? I mean, did you already have that planned?"

His grin was tight. "I've been carrying this damned ring around for the past four months," he said. "Just on the off chance you'd say you were open to it."

She burst into laughter.

"That's still not a yes," he said, and she could see the vulnerability in his eyes.

"That's a yes," she responded, and he got to his feet, kissing the hell out of her. Then he pulled back, slipping the ring on her finger, and kissed her again.

"All right then, future Mrs. Chu," he said, holding her tight, his eyes smoldering. "Let's go get you to your party... and then I'm going to take you home and show you just what your future holds."

Her body thrilled at the thought. "Lead the way," she said, and they walked into their future together.

· ♥ · ♥ · ♥ · ♥ · ♥ ·

Thank you so much for reading Rachel and Ren's story... I hope you've enjoyed reading the Fandom Hearts series as much as I've enjoyed writing it! Feel like reading more geeky rom coms? Try the Ponto Beach Reunion *series. Join the Nerd Herd in their adventures, with plenty of banter, fun, and feels!*

A Note From Cathy

Hi!

Thank you so much for spending time with the love stories from Fandom Hearts! I've loved writing this series, and I hope you've enjoyed reading it. The series is complete (I think? Probably? <g>) If you did enjoy the book, please take a minute to write a review of this on Amazon and Goodreads. Reviews make a huge difference in an author being discovered in book searches and shared with other readers!

But in the meantime, if you're interested in more fun, geeky, diverse rom coms, you might check out the Ponto Beach Reunion series. In high school, they called themselves the Nerd Herd: a group of misfit friends who weathered honors courses, relationships, and teen angst together. The last ten years have taken them in different directions, but their friendships have endured—and evolved. As this tight-knit crew finds their way back to one another through unexpected circumstances, they'll have to navigate old hang-ups and new unresolved feelings. As for falling in love? It isn't on the agenda, but it's not *not* on the agenda either. :)

Enjoy!

Cathy

ABOUT THE AUTHOR

Cathy Yardley writes fun, geeky, and diverse characters who believe that underdogs can make good and sometimes being a little wrong is just right.

She likes writing about quirky, crazy adventures, because she's had plenty of her own: she had her own army in the Society of Creative Anachronism; she's spent a New Year's on a 3-day solitary vision quest in the Mojave Desert; she had VIP access to the Viper Room in Los Angeles.

Now, she spends her time writing in the wilds of Eastern Washington, trying to prevent her son from learning the truth of any of said adventures, and riding herd on her two dogs (and one husband.)

Want to make sure you never miss a release? For news about future titles, sneak peeks, and other fun stuff, please sign up for Cathy's newsletter here.

Let's Get Social!

Hang out in Cathy's Facebook group, Can't Yardley Wait

Talk to Cathy on Twitter

See silly stuff from Cathy's life on Instagram

Never miss a release! Follow on Amazon

Don't miss a sale — follow on BookBub

ALSO BY

THE PONTO BEACH REUNION SERIES

Love, Comment Subscribe

Gouda Friends

Ex Appeal

THE FANDOM HEART SERIES

Level Up

Hooked

One True Pairing

Game of Hearts

What Happens at Con

Ms. Behave

Playing Doctor

Ship of Fools
SMARTYPANTS ROMANCE

Prose Before Bros
STAND ALONE TITLES

The Surfer Solution

Guilty Pleasures

Jack & Jilted

Baby, It's Cold Outside